He didn't look like a high roller.

His jeans and the faded denim shirt he wore didn't sport any designer labels. His watch had a plain black leather strap, after all.

Yet everything about him hinted at power, if not wealth. She'd met few men as coolly self-confident, fewer still with such a hard, muscled body. And while Tracy didn't understand how she'd ended up in Drew's arms last night, she couldn't deny the brief contact had left its mark.

But the sudden quivering low in her belly provided one response, and common sense another. The two of them would go their separate ways after L.A. She'd probably never see him again. Plus, he'd offered to refer her to a shrink. She'd be a fool to hop in the sack with someone who thought she had a screw or two loose.

On the other hand...

Dear Reader,

What better way to keep warm on these brisk November nights than being caught up in the four adrenaline-pumping romances Silhouette Intimate Moments has for you!

USA TODAY bestselling author Merline Lovelace starts off the month with *Closer Encounters* (#1439), the latest installment in her CODE NAME: DANGER miniseries. An undercover agent and a former D.A. must work together, all while fighting a consuming attraction, to solve a sixty-year-old murder. RITA® Award-winning author Catherine Mann continues her WINGMEN WARRIORS series with *Fully Engaged* (#1440). To save a woman from his past, an Air Force warrior must face his worst nightmares.

Popular author Cindy Dees delights us with *The Lost Prince* (#1441), where a Red Cross aide must risk her life and her heart to help an overthrown prince save his crumbling nation. And be sure to read *A Sultan's Ransom* (#1442), the second book in Loreth Anne White's SHADOW SOLDIERS trilogy. Here, a mercenary and a doctor must team up to stop a deadly biological plague from wreaking havoc on the world.

Over the next few months, watch as Silhouette Intimate Moments brings exciting changes to its covers, and look for our new name, Silhouette Romantic Suspense, coming in February 2007. As always, we'll deliver on our promise of breathtaking romance set against a backdrop of suspense. Have a wonderful November, and happy reading!

Sincerely,

Patience Smith
Associate Senior Editor

Please address questions and book requests to:
Silhouette Reader Service
U.S.: 3010 Walden Ave., P.O. Box 1325, Buffalo, NY 14269
Canadian: P.O. Box 609, Fort Erie, Ont. L2A 5X3

MERLINE LOVELACE

Closer Encounters

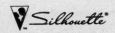

INTIMATE MOMENTS™

Published by Silhouette Books

America's Publisher of Contemporary Romance

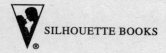 SILHOUETTE BOOKS

ISBN-13: 978-0-373-27509-0
ISBN-10:   0-373-27509-9

CLOSER ENCOUNTERS

Books by Merline Lovelace

Silhouette Intimate Moments

Somewhere in Time #593
*Night of the Jaguar #637
*The Cowboy and the Cossack #657
*Undercover Man #669
*Perfect Double #692
The 14th...and Forever #764
Return to Sender #866
If a Man Answers #878
The Mercenary and the New Mom #908
A Man of His Word #938
Mistaken Identity #987
The Harder They Fall #999
Special Report #1045
   "Final Approach...to Forever"
The Spy Who Loved Him #1052
Twice in a Lifetime #1071
*Hot as Ice #1129
*Texas Hero #1165
*To Love a Thief #1225
A Question of Intent #1255
The Right Stuff #1279
*Diamonds Can Be Deadly #1411
*Closer Encounters #1439

*Code Name: Danger

MERLINE LOVELACE

spent twenty-three years in the U.S. Air Force, pulling tours in Vietnam, at the Pentagon and at bases all over the world. When she hung up her uniform, she decided to try her hand at writing. She now has more than sixty novels published and over seven million copies of her books in print. Merline and her own handsome hero live in Oklahoma. When she's not glued to her keyboard, she loves traveling to exotic locations, chasing little white balls around the golf course and long, lazy dinners with family and friends.

This is for Vernon, my handsome,
curly-haired brother-in-law, who trained
at the Merchant Marine base on Catalina Island.
Like his brother—my own handsome hero—
he served his country with great distinction.

Prologue

November, 1941

The liquid notes soared through the balmy California night. They sprang from the golden slide of two trombones in perfect unison. The reedy seduction of an alto sax. The swish of a steel brush against cymbals. More than fifteen hundred couples lost to the dreamy ballad swayed cheek-to-cheek on the parquet floor of the world famous Avalon Ballroom on Catalina Island.

The singer waited for the clarinet to weep out the final bars of the bridge before stepping up to the mike. Her golden snood glittering in the light from five Tiffany chandeliers, Trixie Halston cradled the mike and poured out a throaty promise to walk alone, saving her laughter and her smiles until she could share them with her love.

She put her heart into each note, her earthy, provocative signature on each phrase. She was good at making every male in the audience think she was singing to him alone. Very good. All the while she scanned the crowd.

Johnny was here. She'd seen him come in a few moments ago, tall and curly-haired and achingly handsome in his merchant marine uniform. He'd come in response to the urgent message she'd left this afternoon. Now she'd lost him in the throng of dancers jamming the ballroom.

Her impatience mounting, she rushed the refrain and earned a quick frown from the bandleader. Smiling an apology, Trixie slowed for the last stanza. When the music faded, she signed off with her signature farewell to the men serving aboard the ships that sailed from Southern California's busy ports.

"Good night to all you mariners. Stay safe."

She didn't need to glance at the note the band's PR director had passed her to add a heartfelt postscript.

"And to the men of the USS *Kallister,* keep a song in your heart."

She often singled out ships for a personal message, but this was Johnny's ship. A munitions ship. Packed with high explosives for British and

Prologue

November, 1941

The liquid notes soared through the balmy California night. They sprang from the golden slide of two trombones in perfect unison. The reedy seduction of an alto sax. The swish of a steel brush against cymbals. More than fifteen hundred couples lost to the dreamy ballad swayed cheek-to-cheek on the parquet floor of the world famous Avalon Ballroom on Catalina Island.

The singer waited for the clarinet to weep out the final bars of the bridge before stepping up to the mike. Her golden snood glittering in the light from five Tiffany chandeliers, Trixie Halston cradled the mike and poured out a throaty promise to walk alone, saving her laughter and her smiles until she could share them with her love.

She put her heart into each note, her earthy, provocative signature on each phrase. She was good at making every male in the audience think she was singing to him alone. Very good. All the while she scanned the crowd.

Johnny was here. She'd seen him come in a few moments ago, tall and curly-haired and achingly handsome in his merchant marine uniform. He'd come in response to the urgent message she'd left this afternoon. Now she'd lost him in the throng of dancers jamming the ballroom.

Her impatience mounting, she rushed the refrain and earned a quick frown from the bandleader. Smiling an apology, Trixie slowed for the last stanza. When the music faded, she signed off with her signature farewell to the men serving aboard the ships that sailed from Southern California's busy ports.

"Good night to all you mariners. Stay safe."

She didn't need to glance at the note the band's PR director had passed her to add a heartfelt postscript.

"And to the men of the USS *Kallister,* keep a song in your heart."

She often singled out ships for a personal message, but this was Johnny's ship. A munitions ship. Packed with high explosives for British and

Australian forces fighting a brutal holding action in the Pacific. The United States had yet to enter the war that was engulfing the rest of the world, but even the most rabid isolationists and antiwar activists acknowledged it was just a matter of months, if not weeks. In the meantime, American ships ran a gauntlet of U-boats lurking off the coasts to supply the Allies with desperately needed supplies purchased under the lend-lease program.

Johnny hadn't said anything about leaving L.A. last night. He couldn't, of course. Yet Trixie guessed he must be shipping out soon. His kisses had been more urgent, his embrace more passionate, as if he wanted to imprint the feel of her, the taste of her, on his memory.

Anxious to get to him, she accepted the thunderous applause and slipped behind the stage curtains. A door led directly outdoors and onto the balcony that ringed the upper story ballroom.

Waves slapped against the rocks five stories below. The breeze carried the gay tinkle of rigging from the boats rocking at anchor in Avalon Harbor. Eager, impatient, Trixie called her lover's name.

"Johnny?"

She heard a movement in one of the alcoves framed by the balcony's ornate Moorish arches. With joy in her heart, she spun toward the sound.

That's all she had. One instant of eager anticipation. Then an arm thrust out of the darkness and slammed into her shoulder. Off balance in her thick-soled platform wedgies, Trixie fell against the railing.

"Johnny!"

Another shove sent her over the rail. A scream ripping from her throat, she plummeted to the rocks below.

Chapter 1

November, present day

An early frost glittered on the naked limbs of the chestnut trees lining the quiet side street just off Massachusetts Avenue, in the heart of Washington, D.C.'s, embassy district. Commuters pouring out of the Metro stop at the corner kept their heads down against the biting wind as they hurried to work.

If any had happened to glance at the elegant three-story town house halfway down the block, they might have noticed the discreet bronze plaque beside the door. The plaque indicated the structure housed the offices of the President's Special Envoy.

The title was held by Nick Jensen, a jet-setting restaurateur who owned a string of exclusive watering holes that catered to the rich and famous around the world. Only a handful of Washington insiders knew that title masked Jensen's real job—director of OMEGA. The small, ultrasecret organization sent its operatives into the field only at the request of the president himself.

One of those agents had just been activated.

Andrew McDowell—code name Riever—sat at the briefing table in the high-tech control center on the top floor of the town house. Shielded from penetration by every electronic eavesdropping device known to man, the control center hummed with the pulse of OMEGA's heartbeat.

Frowning, Drew skimmed the data projected onto the screen taking up almost the whole north wall. There wasn't much to skim. Just a list of Internet queries seeking information on the USS *Kallister*. Several of the queries cited a sailing date of 15 November and requested information on the ship's course and cargo. The problem was, that course was classified. So was the cargo in the hold of the refurbished WWII-era ship.

The rust bucket that had hauled explosives across the Pacific during the war had been torpedoed and almost sunk. Mothballed after the war, it had been refitted and recommissioned in the late '60s to meet the escalating demands of the Vietnam conflict.

Now it carried a secret cargo—so secret, every circuit at the White House situation room had popped when the vigilant watchdogs at NSA plucked this string of queries out of the billions their computers screened every day.

"What do you think, Riever?"

Drew had derived his code name from the fierce raiders who wreaked such havoc on the Anglo-Scottish border in past centuries. Like his long-ago ancestors, he was hawk-eyed and broad-shouldered enough to swing a claymore. He felt the urge to swing one now.

He'd served a hitch in the navy before being recruited by OMEGA. That was almost eight years ago, but there was enough of the sailor left in him to generate a cold, deadly fury at the possibility someone might deliberately put a U.S. vessel at risk.

"I think," he said to his boss, "I'd better haul my ass out to the west coast and check out the female who generated these queries. What have we got on her so far?"

"Not much," Nick Jensen replied. Tall, tanned and tawny-haired, the one-time agent with the code name Lightning nodded to the console operator. A click of a mouse brought up the digitized image of a Washington state driver's license.

According to the DMV, Tracy Brandt was twenty-eight years old, stood five-six and weighed a respectable one hundred and thirty-two pounds. No anorexic toothpick there.

The camera must have caught Brandt by surprise.

Her picture showed a brunette with startled green eyes and a light dusting of freckles across the bridge of her nose.

"Ms. Brandt worked as a budget analyst at the Puget Sound shipyards until two weeks ago," Lightning advised Drew. "Her supervisor says he fired her because of repeated absences from work. He also says she told him he'd be sorry for letting her go."

Uh-oh. A defensive employee fired for cause. Talk about your basic formula for disaster.

"What about her security clearances?"

"She crunched payroll numbers. Nothing that required a top-secret clearance. Certainly nothing that would give her access to the cargo packed in the hold of the *Kallister*."

Lightning drummed his fingers on the table. He knew what the *Kallister* was hauling. He was one of a very small, very select circle who did.

"Brandt's address checks to an apartment complex in Puget Sound, but the electronic queries emanated from Southern California. An Internet café on Catalina Island, to be specific."

"What's she doing there?"

"That's what you're going to find out. She used her Visa to check into the Bella Vista Inn. We got the manager to move out the folks in the room next to hers. He's holding it for you."

A thin smile stretched Drew's lips. With the array of electronic gadgetry available to OMEGA agents,

Ms. Brandt had better watch what she said or did, even in the privacy of her bedroom.

"We're sending a team to Puget Sound to talk to her former coworkers," Lightning advised. "We'll let you know what, if anything, they turn up."

"Roger that."

Lightning's nod encompassed the blonde on the other side of the table. "Denise will act as your controller here at headquarters."

A former Secret Service agent, Denise Kowalski had pumped a bullet into the man she believed was attacking the vice president. The veep had actually been another OMEGA agent in disguise, but Denise's cool head had so impressed everyone involved that the director at the time had requested she be transferred to OMEGA. Drew couldn't think of anyone he'd rather have as his controller.

"Let us know when you make contact with the target," Lightning instructed. "I need to advise the president."

"Will do."

Shoving back his chair, Drew took the stairs to the field dress unit. The wizards in FDU fitted him with an array of sophisticated communications devices and a .45-caliber Glock they'd regripped especially for his hand. After a final session with Denise to work out a reporting schedule, he departed the town house via a hidden back exit. A half hour later he was on his way to sun-drenched Southern California.

* * *

Given the time change, it was barely noon when he landed at LAX, rented a car and drove south to Dana Point. From there it was a forty-minute hydrofoil trip to Catalina, some twenty-six miles off the coast.

The hydrofoil docked in the town of Avalon. Surrounded by steep mountains, the tiny resort snuggled up to a crescent-shaped harbor crowded with fishing boats, cabin cruisers and sleek sailboats. A tall round building with a red roof stood on a spit of rock at the north end of the harbor. Drew's tourist map identified it as the Avalon Casino, the '30s-era movie theater and ballroom that constituted the island's premier tourist attraction.

He'd already been warned that vehicle traffic was restricted on Catalina. Residents depended mainly on golf carts as the primary mode of transportation. Several carts were waiting at the dock to perform taxi service, but Drew opted to heft his carryall and follow a paved walkway to the center of town. A zigzagging side street led up a steep hill to the Bella Vista Inn.

It was a Victorian whimsy set high above the bay. The wraparound porch gave a sweeping view of the hills, the harbor and the casino. Riever accepted an old-fashioned iron key and climbed a winding staircase to the second floor room labeled "Seagull Suite."

The reason for the label became apparent the moment he stepped out onto the suite's minuscule balcony. Gulls squawked and circled overhead. One particularly intrepid creature swooped onto the wooden railing and hopped to within a foot of Drew.

"Sorry, pal. I don't have anything for you."

The gull ruffled his feathers and danced another inch or two, head cocked expectantly. Like most sailors, Drew wasn't particularly fond of gulls and the messes they deposited on gleaming steel decks. This one was nothing if not persistent, however.

"Okay, okay. Let me check out the minibar."

He was tossing honey-roasted cashews to the gull when he spotted his target. She came out the front door of the inn and paused on the porch to zip up a pea-green windbreaker before starting down toward town. Riever smothered an oath, chucked the last of the cashews to the gull and went after her.

Tracy had no idea why she felt so compelled to take another tour of the Avalon Casino. She'd visited it yesterday, shortly after arriving on Catalina, and really didn't have time for a repeat visit. She'd traveled to the island on very private, very wrenching business.

She should get on with it, she thought with a little ache just under her ribs. Once it was done, she'd take the ferry back to the mainland, fly home to Washington and start looking for another job.

God knew she needed one. Her savings account was empty and she had less than two hundred dollars in her checking account. Thank goodness for credit cards, although she'd already maxed out two and was nudging close to the limit on her third. The finance company had repossessed her car last month, which had made getting back and forth to work a challenge. When she still had a job to get to, that is.

Her boss should have understood, she thought indignantly. Or at least been more sympathetic to her situation. She'd worked her butt off for the guy for almost six years. And covered *his* butt on more than one occasion! Yet when her vacation time had run out and she'd been forced to ask for leave without pay, the bastard had told her to choose between her job and Jack.

The ache just under her ribs intensified and seeped into her heart, drop by painful drop. She couldn't believe Jack had really left her. He'd been the only man in her life for so long. Her only friend. Her only family.

Racked by a loneliness that went bone deep, Tracy shoved her hands in the pockets of her pistachio-colored windbreaker and followed the cobbled walk that circled the harbor. November was a little too late in the year for swimmers, but a few determined sun-worshippers had spread towels on the beach and were soaking up rays. Other tourists strolled the pedestrians-only main boulevard. A blend of old Mexico and California chic, the street was lined with shops, restaurants and tall, swaying palms.

Head down, shoulders hunched, Tracy barely

glanced at the shop windows. Her destination was the stucco arch at the far end of Crescent Avenue. The arch formed the entrance to another paved walk. This path led to the casino, which stood in majestic splendor at the north end of the harbor.

As Tracy had learned during her tour yesterday, the fabled Avalon Casino had nothing to do with gambling. The label derived from the Italian word for gathering place or festive area, and that's certainly what this structure had been designed for. The spectacular first-floor theater could seat twelve hundred avid movie buffs. Twice as many couples could dance the night away in the magnificent upper-story ballroom. So brilliantly illuminated at night that it could be seen from the mainland, the Avalon Casino had lured visitors since it first opened in 1929.

Just as it lured Tracy now.

It was weird, this urge that pulled her back to the place. Almost as weird as the tune that kept drifting through her head. She'd first heard the slow, plaintive melody during the tour yesterday. So faint, she'd caught only a few bars. So sad, it had seemed to echo her personal misery.

She'd thought at first the music had drifted up to the ballroom from one of the boats moored in the harbor below. Then she decided it was probably piped in as background for the tour, designed to evoke a feeling for the poignant ballads of the big band era.

The odd thing was that no else seemed to have

heard it. The rest of her group had trailed after the guide, oohing and aahing over the ballroom's massive Tiffany chandeliers, art deco wall sconces and vast parquet floor cushioned by a resilient cork mat to ease the aching feet of four thousand jitterbuggers.

Deciding it was just her overactive imagination at work, Tracy had finished the tour and walked back toward town. To her consternation, the melody accompanied her, wandering in and out of her head as if it were lost. Only this time, snatches of lyrics came with them. Something about waiting, about gathering dreams, about walking alone until...

Until what?

Haunted by the tune, she'd stopped at an Internet café and spent dollars she couldn't afford to Google the phrases. One query led to another, then another.

She now knew "I'll Walk Alone" was both the title and the theme of a big band hit sung by all the great female singers of the late '30s and early '40s, including Billie Holiday, Dinah Shore and Trixie Halston—who'd died in a tragic accident right here at the Avalon Casino.

What she didn't know was why she couldn't get the song out of her head!

It was there now, calling to her, beckoning to her, luring her like the sirens of old had lured unwary sailors to their death. She could hear it as she stood in line at the box office to purchase a tour ticket.

"You just made it."

Tracy blinked, sure the woman in the old-fashioned glass booth had spoken to her. Her lips had moved. Her smile invited a reply. But the music had drowned her out.

"I'm sorry. What did you say?"

"I said you just made it. The last tour of the day starts in two minutes."

Tracy slid her charge card through the opening in the glass and held her breath until it went through. She hadn't maxed this one out yet, thank goodness. She signed the slip, took her ticket and turned—only to collide with the man in line behind her.

"Sorry!"

"No problem."

Too absorbed by the haunting melody to note more than an easy smile and gold-flecked hazel eyes, she nodded absently and joined the tourists now streaming into the casino.

Yesterday, the lobby's solid black-walnut wall panels and glorious red-arched ceiling had taken her breath away. Today she could barely contain her impatience as the tour guide explained the casino's history and unique engineering. Once inside the theater, not even the immense proscenium arch and murals glittering with silver and gold foil could hold her attention. Nor could the booming notes of the Page pipe organ that had added drama to the silent movies shown in the theater drown out the song inside Tracy's head.

The music was louder now, the lyrics more distinct. She'd printed out a copy after Googling them up yesterday, and knew them almost by heart. Each note was a sigh, each word a promise. They called to her, urging her upstairs to the ballroom.

Her heart pounded as the tour guide led the group to the set of spiral ramps so many eager couples had ascended during the swing era. The guide took the ramps slowly, in deference to the older members in the group, and paused at the lounge halfway up to let them rest and view the black-and-white photos of the bands that had played the Avalon Ballroom.

Tracy's pulse kicked up another notch as she skimmed over photos of bands led by Artie Shaw, Harry James and Russ Morgan. Suddenly, her breath stopped in her throat.

There! That was Kenny Jones swinging a baton in front of his orchestra. And the woman at the microphone. Trixie Halston. Tracy recognized the singer from the photos she'd pulled up yesterday. As she stared at the slender chanteuse with her dark hair styled in a peekaboo sweep, the music inside her head grew louder, the notes more urgent.

Determined to get the damned song out of her head, Tracy slipped away from the group and hit the next incline. Her breath came faster with each step. Her blood thundered in her ears.

She took the last ramp at a near run and burst into

the cavernous ballroom. The music swelled to an angry crescendo, pulling her across the parquet floor, past the empty stage and through one of the Moorish arches onto the balcony.

Eyes wild, heart hammering, Tracy leaned over the stucco wall ringing the balcony. Waves foamed against the rocks below. The sun had disappeared behind the mountains, leaving the sea looking cold and gray. Like death, she thought, gripped by a sudden, icy panic.

Panic turned to terror as an unseen force thumped her hard between the shoulder blades.

Chapter 2

"**I**'ve got you!"

Fisting his hand in the folds of his target's pea-green windbreaker, Drew yanked her backward. She fell against him. Hard. Her butt slammed his thigh. Her hipbone gouged into his groin.

Grunting, he held on to her until she righted herself. But he wasn't too happy with Ms. Brandt when she whirled around and stared at him with wild eyes. Still feeling the imprint of that hip, he released her.

"What the hell were you doing, leaning over the rail like that?"

His snarl drained what little color she had left in her face. She shrank away and bumped up against the rail again. Cursing, Drew got another grip on her windbreaker.

"Hey! Careful! It's a long way down."

That penetrated, thank God. Locking both hands on his wrist, she threw a frantic glance over her shoulder. A cold breeze set the ends of her mink-brown hair to dancing. Drew felt its bite as a series of shudders wracked the woman.

When the shivers subsided, she blinked several times and eased upright. Drew maintained his grip, just in case. It *was* a long way down and Tracy Brandt's face was still pretty much the color of her jacket.

"You okay?" he asked.

"I… I think so."

Drew didn't release her until she put a good three feet between her and the ledge.

"What happened?"

"I got a little dizzy." She rubbed her temple with a shaking hand. "The music… It was so loud."

"Music?"

"You didn't hear it?" The wild look came back into her eyes. "The melody? The lyrics?"

He hadn't heard anything but the drum of his blood after he'd watched her slip away from the group. She'd acted so furtive his hunting instincts had kicked in big-time and the thrill of the chase had thrummed in his ears. He could hardly admit that to his prey, however.

"No, I didn't hear any music." Wondering if he

were dealing with a nutcase here, Drew asked warily, "Do you still hear it?"

A crease appeared between her eyebrows as she cocked her head and listened. Her intense concentration gave him ample time to compare Ms. Brandt in the flesh to the Ms. Brandt captured by the cameras of the Washington driver's license division.

The eyes were the same misty green. The freckles were still there, a faint spackling across the bridge of her nose and her cheeks. Her hair was longer than in the photo. A tumble of dark brown, the silky mass just brushed her shoulders. Although the features were essentially the same, their setting had changed. There were dark smudges under her eyes and her face appeared thinner. Much thinner.

So did the rest of her. Her license had tagged her at one thirty-two. She didn't look anywhere close to that. The loose windbreaker concealed most of her upper torso, but he'd had plenty of opportunity to observe the lower portion as he'd trudged up the ramps behind her. Her jeans hugged a tight, trim rear. Her slender thighs looked as though they'd wrap perfectly around a man.

Too bad he wouldn't get the chance to test that supposition. For one thing, Tracy Brandt was his target. For another, the woman heard voices in her head.

Or had. Apparently she wasn't hearing them any longer. Looking uncomfortable, she admitted as much and fumbled for an explanation of her erratic behavior.

"I guess I'm just a little stressed."

Losing a job would stress anyone, Drew thought. So would messing with highly classified information you weren't supposed to have access to.

A loud rumble from the vicinity of her stomach interrupted his thoughts and drew an embarrassed laugh from her.

"Or maybe it's just hunger. I missed lunch."

She'd just handed Drew the perfect opening. "Then we'd better get you something to eat."

"Thanks, but you're on the tour. I'll just head back down on my own and—"

"Those ramps are steep. You might get wobbly again. I'll walk down with you."

"Really, I'm fine. You don't have to cut short your tour on my account."

Ignoring her protests, he took her elbow and steered her back through the Moorish arch. The rest of the group was just entering the ballroom. The guide looked distinctly displeased with their temporary absence.

"I must ask you not to wander off on your own like that."

"My friend felt dizzy and needed air," Drew explained calmy. "I'm going to take her down. Thanks for the very informative tour."

His grip remained firm as they exited the ballroom. A fierce satisfaction hummed through him. He couldn't remember the last time a prey had fallen into his hands so easily and conveniently.

"My name's Andrew, by the way. Andrew McDowell. Drew to my friends."

"Tracy Brandt."

"Where's home, Tracy?"

"Puget Sound, Washington. For now, anyway."

Drew kept it casual. "You're moving?"

"Maybe. I don't know."

He cocked an eyebrow, but she dodged the implied question with a small shrug. "It's a long story. Not worth boring a stranger with."

Baby, you've got that wrong! Hiding a sardonic smile, Drew helped her negotiate the sloping ramps. Once outside, he released her elbow. Her cheeks were still pale, making the shadows under her eyes stand out in stark relief, but she seemed to revive in the brisk salt air.

"Do you like seafood?" Drew asked.

She angled her head and gave him a smile. A real one, he saw, surprised at the way it transformed her face.

"What kind of a question is that to ask someone from Puget Sound?"

"My mistake. The restaurant at the inn where I'm staying supposedly does a great grilled tilapia. At least according to the manager of the Bella Vista."

"You're staying at the Bella Vista? So am I."

"There you go, then. We're neighbors. Want to give the tilapia a shot or have you already tried it?"

"No, I haven't."

Tracy hesitated, chewing on her lower lip. She couldn't afford to rack up a bill at the inn's fancy restaurant. The only reason she'd stayed at the Bella Vista was because it offered a modified American plan that included a continental breakfast. Unfortunately, she'd been too wired this morning to down more than coffee and half a blueberry muffin. She needed to eat something soon or she'd make a fool of herself—again!—by keeling over at this man's feet.

"I'm not really dressed for a nice restaurant. I saw a place out on the pier that serves fish and chips. We could try that."

"The pier it is," he said easily.

Catalina's Green Pier jutted into the harbor from midpoint on Avalon's narrow, sandy beach. It got its name from the green-painted structure perched in the center of the pier. According to a tourist brochure Tracy had read, the wooden building, with its dazzling white trim and distinctive clock tower, was the island's second most recognizable landmark after the casino. Originally a fish market, it now housed the official weigh station for sport fishermen, souvenir shops and eateries.

To Tracy's secret relief, her escort insisted on paying for their meal. They ate in the open air, carrying their soft drinks and red plastic baskets to a long wooden table with an unobstructed view of the circular harbor and the town that hugged it. As advertised, the fish was crunchy on the outside, deliciously moist and flaky inside. The French fries and hush puppies were steaming hot. Tracy burned the inside of her mouth on the first bite, yet had to fight to keep from scarfing down another.

"This is nice," Drew commented, his gaze skimming over the boats rocking gently on the swells.

"Yes, it is."

Those scary moments on the casino balcony faded as Tracy munched on her hush puppy and drank in the scene. The late afternoon shadows had deepened into an early evening dusk. Lights were beginning to twinkle on in the shops and houses that stair-stepped up the steep hills surrounding the bay. The breeze had died and the temperature hovered at a comfortable sixty-five or so. The scene was so calm, so idyllic. Just as Jack had described it.

"Very nice," she murmured with a hitch in her voice that matched the one in her heart.

Dunking a fry in ketchup, she pushed it around and waited for the ache to pass. When she looked up, she found Drew watching her with a question in his eyes.

They were really sexy eyes, Tracy decided, a palette of gold and brown and green framed by lashes the same color as the mahogany streaks in his dark hair. She liked the face they were set in, too. She wouldn't qualify it as handsome, exactly. More rugged-looking, with a strong chin and tanned skin that suggested he spent more time outdoors than in.

With his broad shoulders and lean, athletic body, he didn't look the type to go in for salon tanning sessions.

Not that Tracy was any judge of type. Except for Jack, her relationships with the male species had been brief and somewhat less than satisfactory.

The thought made the ache sharper, until it lanced into her like vicious little shards. It took an act of sheer will to respond to Drew's silent query.

"A friend of mine used to come here years ago. He fell in love with the place and talked all the time about coming back."

"Why didn't he?"

"I guess... I guess he just never got around to it."

She couldn't talk about Jack. The hurt was too raw, too private. Scanning the harbor, she latched on to a sleek white yacht as a change of topic.

"Look at that. What do you suppose something like that costs?"

"More than either of us could afford."

The drawled response piqued Tracy's curiosity. All she knew about this man was his name and that he had really sexy eyes. She glanced down and saw he wasn't wearing a wedding ring. That didn't mean anything, of course, but it gave her the incentive to pry a little.

"Where's home for you, Drew?"

"I live in Virginia, about an hour south of D.C."

"What do you do?"

"My father-in-law and I own and operate a chain of shops that specialize in classic car restoration."

Well, that settled the question of his marital status. Tracy was battling an absurd sense of disappointment when her dinner companion added a clarification.

"Actually, Charlie is my ex-father-in-law. I met his daughter some years back. I was in the navy then, and it took Joyce all of eight months to decide being a sailor's wife wasn't her thing. Not this particular sailor's wife, anyway."

She didn't detect any hurt in his crooked grin. Only a self-deprecating chagrin.

"I take it the divorce didn't damage your relationship with your wife's father."

"Just the opposite. Charlie was as relieved as Joyce when we split. He saw how upset she got when I had to pull sea duty."

Upset wasn't quite the right word for it, Drew thought wryly. His high-strung, temperamental wife had pitched a world-class fit every time he'd had to pack his sea bag. Short of going AWOL, all Drew could do was promise to leave the navy when his hitch was up.

Joyce had decided to leave him instead. Drew had never admitted it to anyone, but he'd been every bit as relieved as his father-in-law when she'd filed for divorce.

"Charlie and I always got along well," he said with a shrug. "So well he asked me to join him in his business when I left the navy."

Their partnership had proved far more enduring

and satisfying than his marriage. Drew had already been recruited by OMEGA and needed a base of operations that would allow him to come and go at will. Charlie had been happy to turn over most of the traveling to classic car conventions and searches for rare parts to his partner.

Drew knew Charlie suspected his business partner did more than shop for parts during those travels, but the old man had never asked about the extended absences. The fact that Drew had helped grow Classic Motors, Inc. into a nationwide chain of highly profitable shops might have had something to do with Charlie's reticence.

"What about you?" he asked, getting back to the business that had sent him on this particular trip. "What do you do?"

"I worked as a budget analyst for a defense contractor in Puget Sound until recently."

He waited, wondering if she'd admit she'd been fired. When she didn't, he applied the screws.

"Why did you leave?"

"It was, uh, time to look for something better." With a show of nonchalance, she nodded to the sleek white yacht. "Who knows, maybe I'll land something that pays enough to afford one of those."

"Yeah," he drawled, "who knows?"

Drew had spent almost six years as an undercover operative. In that time he'd taken down his share of drug dealers, black marketers and other scum who trafficked in human misery. He'd learned the hard way that greed had some ugly faces. Real ugly. Even the so-called religious fanatics who blew themselves up or bombed abortion clinics in the name of God were motivated by a sadistic hunger for dominance and power.

In Drew's considered opinion, the bastards who sold their country's secrets were among the worst of the lot. Their avarice put the lives of countless innocent citizens at risk. He had no evidence Tracy Brandt intended to sell classified information. He still hadn't ascertained what, if any, information about the USS *Kallister* and its cargo she may have acquired.

But he would, he vowed. He would.

Infusing his voice with a sympathy he was far from feeling, he tightened the screws a little more.

"It's tough to be out of work, but you can't let it get to you. Or make you do something crazy."

"Crazy?"

"Like up there," he said, jerking his chin toward the round casino building now lit up like a beacon. "On that balcony."

Her jaw dropped. Goggle-eyed, she gaped at him for several seconds. "You think…? You think I intended to *jump?*"

"Kind of looked that way from where I was standing."

"I had no intention of jumping!" Indignation put spots of red in her cheeks and lit sparks in her green eyes. "I told you, it was the music…. It made feel me dizzy and disoriented."

"Right. The music."

Her flushed deepened to a rosy brick. "Or, as I said, I might just have been hungry. We've taken care of that problem, so you don't have to worry that I'll jump off the pier and you'll have to dive in after me."

"No need to get riled. I was just trying to help."

"Yes, well… Thanks." Her feathers thoroughly ruffled, she swung off the bench, scooped up her plastic basket and tossed it in the trash. "And thanks for dinner. I'll leave you to enjoy the rest of yours."

"I'm done," Drew replied, swinging a leg over the bench. "I'll walk back to the inn with you."

"I'm not going back to the inn. Not just yet. Have a nice time on Catalina, Mr. McDowell."

Drew trailed her to an Internet café tucked between two souvenir shops. Ignoring the coffee bar, she made a beeline for a computer and inserted a credit card. Mere moments later she was hunched over the screen and clicking away on the keyboard.

Keeping her in his line of sight, Drew chose an isolated bench well away from the glow of shop windows and extracted his cell phone. It was one of those ultrathin, ultraexpensive models that could do everything but flush the toilet. Drew figured the wizards who worked for Lightning's wife, Mackenzie

Blair, had probably packed it with enough souped-up circuitry to do that, too, if necessary.

Lounging on the bench like a patient tourist waiting for his souvenir-hunting spouse, he pressed a quick-dial button and was instantly connected via secure satellite to OMEGA headquarters. Standard protocol required Drew to be identified via voiceprint and code name before his controller responded. A recent case worked by a fellow operative, Jordan Colby, had added an iris scan to the process.

"This is Riever," he said, aiming the phone's built-in camera at his right eye.

Drew waited for another second or two until Denise Kowalski got the green light indicating the caller's iris scan and voiceprint matched those on file for Drew McDowell.

"I read you." Her image appeared on the phone's screen. "How's it going?"

"So far, so good. I'm in place and have established contact with the target. Matter of fact, we just had dinner together."

The former Secret Service agent raised a sandy eyebrow. "That's fast work, Riever, even for you."

"The pace picked up in a hurry right after I got here."

Keeping an eye on the dark head bent over the computer, he relayed the events of the afternoon and evening.

"She insists she wasn't going to jump, but it's hard to take the word of someone who hears voices. Check her medical records for me, will you? See if there's anything else going on in her head besides singing."

"Will do."

"We also need to get linked into the Chocolate Cyberchip Café. She's in there now, plugging away."

"Already done. That's the same site she used yesterday to make all those queries about the *Kallister*. Hang loose while I check with comm to see if they're picking up her signals."

Denise was back a few moments later.

"Comm has her. She's tapped into one of those online music sites. Have a listen."

Drew heard the slide of a trombone followed by a few bars of a reedy sax. Then a female crooned into his ear. Her voice was low and throaty and seductive, like a golden ribbon spooling out onto black satin sheets. Drew almost got hard just listening to her.

"Who the heck is that?"

"Comm says the singer is Trixie Halston. The song is one she recorded in the early forties. 'I'll Walk Alone.' Hmm, the target is playing the same song over again. Wonder why she's so fascinated with it?"

"Good question. See what you can find out about the singer." A sudden movement had Drew signing off. "The target's moving. I'll contact you later."

"Roger that."

Slipping his phone into his pocket, he followed Tracy up to the inn. To his surprise, he could still hear the echo of that smoky, sexy contralto.

Okay, so maybe his target wasn't a couple of bricks shy of a full load. Maybe the song had just stuck in her head, like it had in his. The melody was liquid and smooth, the lyrics simple and repeatable. Drew was humming them under his breath when Tracy disappeared inside the inn.

Once she was inside her room, Drew entered his. His first order of business was to attach a small, almost transparent disk on the wall between their two rooms. The communications gurus had assured him the minuscule listening device could pick up a sneeze on a street corner in Gdansk.

When he screwed a wireless receiver into his ear, Drew heard no sneezes, Polish or otherwise, just the sound of gushing water punctuated by a series of irate mutters.

"Jerk!"

A tap squealed. The water gushed faster.

"How could he think I was going to jump?"

Another squeal, followed by another mutter.

"Do I *look* that pathetic?"

No, Drew wouldn't classify her as pathetic. Weird, maybe. Suspect, certainly. Fingering the earpiece, he adjusted the volume. A bird's-eye view of Avalon's twinkling lights lured him out onto the balcony.

Leaning his elbows on the rail, he listened to the splash that heralded his target's immersion in one of the inn's old-fashioned claw foot tubs. Her long, drawn-out *ahhh* evoked images of bubbles and rising steam. The squish of something wet and spongy evoked another image altogether.

Drew could almost see a wet washcloth sliding over Tracy Brandt's breasts and belly. Despite the cool night air, he started to sweat. From what he'd seen of her under that baggy windbreaker, the woman came equipped with a nice set of curves.

He'd worked his way into a serious consideration of those curves when a squawk jerked him from Tracy's bathroom to his night-wrapped balcony. The gull landed less than a foot from his elbow.

"Hey, fella. You're out late."

Yeah, the bird's cocked head seemed to say. So feed me.

"Okay, okay. Just hold on to your tail feathers."

Halfway to the minibar he heard a scream from the next room. Drew had charged for the door even before his supersensitive mike telegraphed the crack of breaking glass.

Chapter 3

Straining to pick up some sound from inside the target's room, Drew rapped his knuckles on her door.

"Tracy?"

He waited a beat, his mind conjuring a dozen different scenarios, and rapped again.

"Tracy, it's Drew."

He was about to put his shoulder to the oak panel when the lock snicked and the door opened a crack. Cool air whooshed out, then a pale face topped by a towel turban appeared.

"Are you okay?" Drew asked sharply.

"I... I..."

The fumbling response upped his pucker factor another few notches. What the hell had she done?

"The walls are thin," he said with only slight exaggeration. They *were* thin—especially with a high-tech listening device transmitting every decibel of sound.

"I heard a scream and the sound of glass breaking. Are you all right?"

She put a shaking hand to her temple. "I think so."

"What happened?"

"I, uh, dropped something."

She scrunched her forehead, as if trying to remember what. Worried that she'd fallen and whapped her head, Drew softened his tone.

"Something's obviously shaken you. Why don't you unhook the chain and tell me about it?"

She peered through the crack for another second or two, still confused, still hesitant. While she debated, Drew angled his body to one side and surreptitiously removed his earpiece. One way or another, he was getting in to that room.

"Let me in, Tracy. I want to make sure you're okay."

The combination of brisk command and gentle persuasion produced results. The door closed, the chain rattled and Drew stepped inside.

Her rooms were smaller than his. A good deal chillier, too, with the breeze blowing in through the open windows. The view was incredible, but Drew spared the brilliantly illuminated casino framed by those windows barely a glance. His quick, intense scrutiny swept over a combination bedroom/sitting area done in brass and flowery chintzes. He spotted no bloodstains, no overturned furniture, no shattered windows.

The bathroom, on the other hand, looked as though a tornado had just roared through it. Wet towels were strewn everywhere. The entire contents of a cosmetic bag had been dumped on the counter. Glistening glass shards decorated the floor tiles.

Drew eyed them, his gut tightening. Had she dropped that drinking glass by accident? Or was the breakage deliberate, a prelude to slit wrists?

His thoughts grim, he faced the target. She appeared to be recovering from whatever had hit her. The dazed look was gone, anyway. Playing with the belt of her lemon-colored chenille robe, she offered an embarrassed smile.

"The mirror got all clouded with steam. I used my sleeve to clean it and knocked the drinking cup off the counter."

That accounted for the shattered glass. Not the cry that preceded it.

"Did something startle you? I could swear I heard you scream just before the glass broke."

"Was I that loud? I thought I just let out a small squeak."

Small was in the ear of the beholder. Wondering if the ultrasensitive listening device had made him overreact, Drew shrugged.

"Maybe it was just a squeak. But something must have generated it."

"Something did." Her smile went from embarrassed to chagrined. "After I cleared away the steam, I got a good look at this face in the mirror."

"Excuse me?"

"Don't tell me you can't see the bags under these eyes! And this hair."

Tugging off the turban, she raked her hand through the strands of dark mink.

"Look at it! As straight as a board. Not the slightest hint of a wave or a roll. I *have* to get my hands on some bobby pins."

Bobby pins? Drew had a hazy memory of his grandmother with her head hard-wired into tight curls, but had no idea women still stabbed those sharp little implements into their scalps.

He found Brandt's sudden determination to acquire some reassuring, though. If she was so worried about her appearance, odds were she hadn't been planning to slash her wrists. Judging by the angry mutters he'd heard just before she'd climbed into the tub, she evidently hadn't intended to jump off the ballroom balcony, either.

Okay, maybe she wasn't suicidal. Just strange. And mercurial as hell. For a few moments there on the pier, her shoulders had drooped with weariness and sadness shadowed her eyes. Now she seemed gripped by a sort of quivering energy.

"Do you want to go with me?" she asked eagerly.

"Go where?"

"To a drugstore, to buy some bobby pins."

"Now?"

She flipped the ends of her wet hair. "I have to do *something* with this floor mop. Besides, the night's young. How about I tie on a kerchief and we see what's playing at the Roxy? Or grab a stool at the soda fountain and split a dusty miller? It's been ages since I dug a spoon into one of those!"

Drew didn't have a clue what a dusty miller was, but he'd dig a spoon into one just to keep his target talking.

"Sure, I'll go with you."

"Great! I'll get dressed and meet you downstairs. Ten minutes?"

Drew let himself out, wondering if Ms. Brandt had popped a few pills or snorted something before getting into the tub. She was wired. Most definitely wired.

Her eagerness to get out and have some fun stirred more than a few unpleasant memories. Drew's young wife used to meet him at the door when he dragged in after twelve or fourteen hours performing deck drills. Joyce had spent the day cooped up in what the navy euphemistically referred to as junior enlisted housing and swore she had to get out or she'd go stir-crazy. So Drew had traded his uniform for civvies and duly escorted her to a mall or a movie or to the on-base club. Most often to the club.

Consequently Drew had to work to dredge up a

smile when Tracy floated down the stairs. She appeared to have no problem with *her* smile. It was wide and sparkling and hit him with the same wallop it had earlier. Alive with eagerness, she hooked her arm through his.

"Let's go. I can't wait to dive into that chocolate sundae."

Assuming that was the dusty miller, Drew escorted her out of the inn and down the winding walkway to town. He couldn't quite get a handle on what was so different about her. Maybe it was the hair, tucked into a roll at the base of her neck and accented with a headscarf tied in a jaunty bow. Or the high color in her cheeks. Or her darting gaze that seemed to want to take everything in at once.

"The town sure is dead tonight," she commented, clutching Drew's arm. "Where are all the cars?"

"The streets are too narrow for vehicles. Most everyone gets around in golf carts."

Which she should have known after two days on the island. Puzzling over the inconsistency, Drew let her tug him toward a shop with an old-fashioned Drugstore sign illuminated in green and pink neon.

"Here it is, right where I remember it." Eagerly, she reached for the door latch. Excitement bubbled in her voice. "Come on, let's…"

One step into the shop she stopped dead. Confusion blanked her face.

"Tracy? Something wrong?"

"It's all changed," she said in dismay. "Where's the soda fountain?"

Drew skimmed a glance around the small shop. The stressed wood flooring and framed sepia pictures of Catalina in earlier decades suggested the place had been there a while, but the glass shelves crammed with the usual mix of medications, beauty aids and household items were sleek and strictly utilitarian.

"If there was a soda fountain here, it probably went out with the Edsel."

"Edsel Who?" she asked distractedly.

"The Edsel was a car." Drew wondered how many times he'd had to give the same explanation to folks outside the tight circle of classic car buffs. "A real bomb when it came out in the late '50s, but a collector's dream right now."

"Mmm."

Obviously disinterested in Ford's most famous flop, she meandered down the center aisle. Her gaze roamed the shelves, lingering on different objects. Searching, Drew assumed, for the illusive bobby pins. Halfway down the aisle she stopped in front of a carousel of lipsticks.

"Look at all these colors!"

She plucked out a tube for a closer look just as a teenaged clerk rounded the end of the aisle.

"That's the new Caribbean Calypso line," the clerk announced. "Just came in yesterday. Here, try the Juicy Jamaica Red," she suggested. "It's totally awesome. Tastes good, too. Like papaya or melon or something."

Drew stood to one side while the teen painted a slash of crimson on the back of Tracy's hand.

"Ooh, I love it. I'll take it. And a package of bobby pins."

"They're right here. We've had a real run on them since that episode of *Sex and the City*, when Carrie Bradshaw stuck dozens of black pins in her blond hair."

Drew must have missed that episode—along with every other. Feeling totally out it, he waited while Tracy rummaged through a dizzying array of brushes, combs and hairclips. He got through the tough business of choosing between crinkle style and straight-backed pins okay, but was forced to retreat to the magazine rack while she debated the tough choices of face powder, mascara, eye shadow and lip liner.

After that, she hit the perfume counter. Forehead scrunched in concentration, she sniffed one tester after another while Drew studied her from behind the pages of *Motor Trends* magazine.

Funny, he wouldn't have pegged her as a woman who took perfume and war paint so seriously. Granted, their initial meeting had been dramatic and brief. He still had a lot to learn about Ms. Tracy Brandt…including her interest in the USS *Kallister*, he reminded himself grimly.

Forcing himself to be patient, he waited until she'd spritzed on a sample of something called Midnight

Gardenia and added a small vial to her other purchases. With the delight of a chocoholic who'd been turned loose in a candy store, she carted her selections to the register. Her delight turned to shock after the clerk rang them up.

"That'll be twenty-nine eighteen."

Her jaw dropping, Tracy gaped at the girl. "Twenty-nine *dollars?*"

"And eighteen cents," the teen confirmed, twisting the register's digital screen around to display the total.

"That can't be right."

"Maybe I scanned something twice."

While the clerk peered at the summary on the computerized screen, Tracy dug into the plastic bag and extracted several items. She turned them over and over, searching for the price.

"No wonder you got it wrong. These don't have price tags on them."

"The prices are all bar-coded. Look, this Juicy Jamaica Red scans up at six ninety-nine."

"Seven dollars for *lipstick?*"

The teen shrugged. "We have some products left over from the winter line on sale. Want to see those?"

The prospect of another protracted round of searching and sniffing had Drew reaching for his wallet. "That's okay. We'll take what we have here."

"Not at those prices," Tracy protested.

Suspecting her out-of-work status had a lot to do

with the indignant protest, he tossed a ten and a twenty on the counter.

"Price is no object when it comes to making a pretty woman prettier."

The gallantry was clumsy and heavy-handed but got them out of the drugstore. His companion was still muttering over the cost of the lipstick when they walked out into the night.

The streets had been empty of all but a few tourists before. They were deserted now. As Drew steered Tracy toward the corner, the shop windows behind them went dark. A few seconds later, the souvenir shop across the street dimmed its lights.

"Are we under a blackout?" Tracy asked, clutching her purchases as she glanced around.

"Looks like it, doesn't it? Guess they're just rolling up the streets for the night."

"It's only a little after nine!"

"We're a few weeks ahead of the main tourist season. Avalon probably gets livelier then."

"How strange," she murmured. "And sad. Lights used to blaze here all night long."

"Yeah, that's what the tour guide said."

According to the guide who'd escorted them through the casino this afternoon, Avalon had once rocked. When chewing gum magnate William Wrigley bought Catalina Island in 1919, he made it a training camp for his Chicago Cubs and built a field to match the dimensions of Wrigley Field in

Chicago. The Cubs spring training attracted hosts of eager spectators and sportscasters. Among them was a young Ronald "Dutch" Reagan, who zipped back across the channel in 1931 to take the screen test that changed his profession and his life.

Zane Gray set one of his novels on the island and built a home high on one of the hills above Avalon. Sportsmen like Theodore Roosevelt used to troll the deep blue waters for marlin and sailfish. Betty Grable, Cary Grant, John Wayne and friends regularly yachted over from L.A. to frolic at the great hotels and bars.

Along with the rich and famous came thousands of ordinary folks. Always a shrewd businessman, William Wrigley built the Avalon Casino to lure movie buffs and hepcats. They ferried over by the boatload to view first-run films in the casino's magnificent theater or dance until dawn in the upstairs ballroom.

All that activity came to a screeching halt two days after Pearl Harbor. Declaring the island a military zone, the government shut down all commercial boat traffic. For four years Catalina served as a training site for the merchant marines. The only civilians allowed on the island were the residents who provided essential services to the base.

After the war, Catalina and the city of Avalon never quite regained their glitter and glamour. The big band era was over. The Cubs moved their spring training to Florida. Vastly expanded air travel allowed Hollywood's elite to jet down to Acapulco or over to

Hawaii to play. A few stars still sailed across the channel to party on their sleek yachts, but Natalie Wood's tragic drowning seemed to signal the end of that era, too.

Now the town catered primarily to families who used it for a weekend escape and the cruise ship passengers who thronged to the shops during the day and sailed away at dusk.

"It's nice like this," Drew commented. "No crowds, no hassle."

It was also very convenient. He and Tracy were two strangers thrown together in relative isolation. Playing to that theme, he made a casual suggestion.

"Since it looks like our dirty miller is out..."

"Dusty miller," she corrected glumly.

"Since our dusty miller is apparently out, how about a drink?"

That brightened her up. "A drink sounds good."

"Shall we find a bar or go back to the inn and enjoy the view?"

"Let's go back to the inn." With a last look around the darkened streets, she slid her hand into the crook of his arm. "We'll have a private party."

Drew formulated his game plan on the walk back to the Bella Vista. First a drink. Then some idle conversation. Another drink. A casual mention of the ships that sailed from the busy ports across the channel. A not-so-casual reference to the USS *Kallister*.

At the reminder of his mission, his muscles tightened. The involuntary movement pressed Tracy's arm into his side. She slanted him a quick glance, then snuggled closer. The feel of her high, firm breast against his arm did a serious number on his concentration. The scent that tickled his senses didn't help, either.

Midnight gardenia. It fit her, he decided. Her skin was as smooth and creamy as the waxy petals. And like some exotic, night-blooming plant, she'd opened to reveal a showy flower.

So showy, she couldn't wait to experiment with her purchases. Once back at her room, she waggled a hand toward the minibar.

"Do the honors, will you? I just want to powder my nose and put on some lipstick."

"What'll you have?" Drew asked as she sailed for the bathroom.

"Scotch."

"On the rocks?"

"Why water down good hooch?"

While she wrestled with plastic packaging in the bathroom, Drew moved fast. His first objective was the purse she'd deposited on the bed. The wallet held her driver's license, a couple of credit cards and less than ten dollars in cash. No scribbled phone numbers, no cryptic notes and only one picture of Tracy and an older man grinning at the camera. Her father? Grandfather?

Making a mental note to have Denise run her

family history, Drew flipped open her cell phone. The call log showed no calls received or transmitted since she'd arrived on Catalina yesterday.

He had time to give the small suitcase sitting on a luggage rack at the foot of the bed only a quick look. She obviously wasn't intending a long stay. The weekender contained a neatly folded sweater, a cotton blouse, tan twill slacks and several pairs of cotton panties.

The thump of plastic cartons hitting the bathroom wastebasket announced Tracy's imminent return. Diverting to the minibar, he poured two miniatures of scotch into plastic cups and carried them to the French doors. He doubted she would want to go out onto the balcony after her dizzy spell this afternoon, but the view from inside the room served his purpose just as well.

He could see the faint glow of lights from a cargo ship steaming up the San Pedro Channel. His opening conversational gambit was right there in front of him. Planning his segue from the cargo ship to the *Kallister*, he was ready when Tracy emerged from the bathroom.

"Now I feel more like the real me."

Drew just about dropped the plastic cups. If this was the real Tracy Brandt, all it had taken was a little color to bring her out. The bright red lipstick drew his gaze instantly to full, ripe lips. Subtle shading deepened her eyes to a mysterious jungle-green. Pancake makeup

eradicated the dark circles under them. He had no idea
what she'd done to her skin to make it look so lumines-
cent, but he had to battle the urge to stroke a knuckle
down the smooth curve of her cheek.

Her hair was different, too. She'd taken off her
headscarf and released the thick, silky mass from its
tight roll. Still damp, it now fell in unruly waves to
her shoulders.

The change went more than skin-deep, though.
Drew was still trying to figure it out when she raised
her plastic cup.

"Here's to you and here's to me. May we never
disagree. But if we do…"

Drew hooked an eyebrow and waited for the
punch line. He'd heard variations of this toast that
would make his old buddies in the navy blush. Tracy
kept it clean, ending with a merry laugh.

"Here's to me."

She tossed back a healthy swallow, closed her
eyes and let the scotch slide down her throat. When
her lids fluttered up, she stared at the remaining
liquid in near awe.

"That's prime hooch."

Was retro slang the new thing? Tracy certainly
seemed to be into it.

"That's the second time you used the term *hooch*,"
Drew remarked. "I haven't heard that in a while."

Shrugging, she took another sip. "Hooch, booze,
giggle water. Whatever name you pin on this stuff, it

sure goes down smooth. This Juicy Jamaica Red gives it a different flavor, though. Sort of smoky and fruity at the same time."

She ran her tongue over her upper lip, testing, tasting, then moved to the lower. Drew followed her progress with a sudden tightening in his chest.

Damn! Did the woman have any idea how arousing that slow, deliberate swipe was? Probably, since she tipped him a smile that hovered between teasing and provocative.

"Want a taste?"

Drew's ribs squeezed tighter. Telling himself this was all in the line of duty, he bent his head.

Chapter 4

The kiss was soft and warm and wonderful. Tracy floated on it, enjoying the sensations, savoring the pleasure that eddied through her in gentle waves.

It had been so long since she'd been kissed. Too long, she thought dreamily. Drifting on a cottony cloud of delight, she opened her mouth to the one that settled over hers.

The kiss deepened. A hard arm wrapped around her waist. Her body came into contact with another at several highly erotic pressure points. Delight erupted into pleasure so hot and intense it jolted through her like an electric charge.

Her eyes flew open. Her arms froze in the act of twining around a strong, corded neck.

Good Lord! This wasn't a dream! This wasn't anything *close* to a dream! She was wrapped in the arms of a man she'd met just a few hours ago. Worse—much worse!—she was damned if she could recall how she'd gotten there. Thoroughly flustered, she shoved out of his hold.

"What are you doing?"

Frowning, the handsome stranger shagged a hand through his short-cropped hair. His voice was tight, his apology gruff.

"Sorry. Guess I misread the signals."

What signals? The last thing Tracy remembered with any clarity was suggesting Mr. Andrew McDowell take a flying leap off the Green Pier. Not quite in those words, of course, but for the life of her she couldn't imagine how they'd progressed from that chilly parting to a kiss that darned near melted her bones.

Oh, God! Had the stress of the past few months pushed her over the edge? First her job. Then Jack. Now this. Was she losing it? Making a desperate attempt to hide her incipient panic, she angled her chin.

"I think you'd better leave."

He studied her for several moments, his face unreadable.

"Now," she added with as much authority as she could muster at the moment.

He accepted the dictum with a curt nod. "See you around."

Not if she could help it!

Looking as disgruntled as Tracy now felt, he deposited his plastic cup on the coffee table. The minute the door closed behind him she rushed to flip the dead bolt and fumble the chain into place. Slumping against the door, she put a hand to her mouth.

Tracy could still taste him on her lips, still feel the imprint of his body against hers. The man delivered one heck of a kiss. She'd give him that.

Her fingers came away stained with a greasy red smear. Grimacing, she went in search of a tissue. The chaos in the bathroom made her eyes pop.

Good grief! Surely she hadn't created this war zone!

Her mouth curling in distaste, she surveyed the wet towels, the discarded bathrobe, the soap scum ringing the tub. A messy litter of cosmetics drew her to the tiled counter. Confusion swirled through her as she eyed the unfamiliar bottles, brushes and tubes.

Her usual beauty regimen consisted of a swipe of blush, a little mascara and flavored lip gloss. She rarely wore eye shadow and shied away from bright, garish colors like the lipstick lying uncapped on the counter. And where the heck had those bobby pins come from?

The near panic returned, prickling Tracy's skin with icy goose bumps. She *was* losing it!

Her first instinct was to run. Driven by the wild urge to throw her things in her bag and scurry home to the safety of her cozy apartment, she whirled. Reality intervened before she'd taken more than a step or two.

The ferries didn't operate at night. She couldn't get off the island until morning. More to the point, she had a grim task to perform before she could depart Catalina. She'd put it off too long already.

"Tomorrow," she promised softly, her chest squeezing.

The whispered vow came through Drew's earpiece with Dolby-like clarity.

Tomorrow.

He leaned forward in his chair, elbows on knees, waiting for more. All he heard were the muted but unmistakable sounds of Tracy undressing, followed by a swish of bedcovers. An erotic mental image erupted inside his head as she slid into bed. No surprise, with his blood still singed from that wild kiss.

Where the hell had that come from? Drew hadn't intended anything other than a mere taste. Next thing he knew, he was practically devouring the woman whole. The fact that her mouth had opened so seductively under his was no excuse for losing control of the situation. Drew couldn't remember the last time that had happened.

Come to think of it, he couldn't remember the last time a woman had aroused *and* baffled him as much as this one. Frowning, he waited while she struggled to fall asleep.

Minutes passed as he listened to her roll over. Thump the pillow. Roll over again. After a long, gusting sigh, her breathing evened. Sometime later, it deepened to a soft, regular snuffling.

Drew waited another five minutes before he punched his code into his cell phone and aimed the camera at his right eye. Denise appeared on the video screen a few moments later.

"I read you, Riever. You all tucked in for the night?"

"I'm about to be. Anything on the target's medical history?"

"Her last doctor's visit was eight months ago, to renew her prescription for the patch."

"She quit smoking?"

"Not that kind of patch. This one's for birth control. Very convenient for active women who don't want to worry about taking a pill every day."

Drew tucked that information away. "No consults with a mental health professional?"

"None that I could find. But she's paid out big bucks to a home health-care company over the past six months. I found charges for oxygen, nebulizers, nurses' visits and diabetes test strips. I also found charges at the local Wal-Mart for Ensure and Centrum Silver."

"Sounds like she was taking care of a senior. I found a photo in her wallet of her with an older man.

I'm guessing her grandfather. I was going to ask you to run her family history."

"Already done. She has no living relatives. Parents were killed in a car accident when she was three. The aunt who raised her died while Brandt was in college."

"Have the team up in Puget Sound ask around to see if they can ID this older man."

"Roger that. I'll also have them check out the home health-care company. It has a twenty-four-hour number for emergencies, but the person who answered my call was goosey about releasing information until she checked with her supervisor in the morning."

"Good enough. Maybe we can…"

Drew broke off. Head cocked, he strained to hear the soft sounds in the other room. The low murmurs came in snatches interspersed with breathy sighs.

"Something wrong, Riever?"

"I just picked up sounds from next door. Evidently the target talks in her sleep. Correction, make that sings in her sleep."

It took only a few moments for Drew to recognize the melody.

"She's humming the same tune she played on the computer earlier. Did you find anything on the song or the singer?"

"The song was written in the late thirties and recorded by a dozen different crooners over the years. Trixie Halston, the singer Brandt was listening to tonight, recorded her version in 1940."

The low, seductive humming was like a drug, seeping into Drew's veins, reheating his blood. Distracted by it, he had to force his attention back to Denise.

"Did you find anything on Halston?"

"Yeah, I did. She got her start with a small group in Nebraska and sang with a couple of swing bands before joining the Kenny Jones Orchestra. She was his featured singer from 1939 to 1941...until she took a dive off a balcony, right there on Catalina."

The skin on the back of Drew's neck tightened. His gut told him he knew the answer, but he asked anyway.

"What balcony?"

"The same one our target almost jumped off this afternoon," Denise confirmed. "It happened in November 1941. Kenny Jones and his band were playing to a packed house in the ballroom. The newspaper reports said Halston slipped out to get some air after the last set. They also said she'd been known to smoke a joint or hit the bottle between sets. Apparently both were as common among musicians then as they are now. In any case, the ME ruled her death an accident. There were no witnesses and no evidence to suggest otherwise."

Drew wasn't sure what to make of all this. He didn't believe in coincidences. Leaving matters to chance was a good way to eat a bullet in his line of work. Yet he couldn't figure the connection between Tracy Brandt and the singer she seemed so fixated on. Hell, he couldn't figure the woman at all.

"Maybe Brandt was attempting a copycat dive," Denise suggested. "She read about this Halston woman, got all depressed about being out of work, decided to follow Halston's example and end it all."

"Maybe."

At this point, nothing about the target computed. She was bubbly and almost overly bright one moment, quiet and withdrawn the next. The mood swings sent up red flags, but her vehement denial and angry mutters while running the bathwater indicated she hadn't intended to jump. And Drew still hadn't discovered the reason for her interest in the USS *Kallister*.

Tomorrow, he vowed, echoing her soft promise. Tomorrow he'd get down and heavy with Ms. Tracy Brandt.

He was primed and waiting when she came downstairs the next morning. The inn served breakfast in a sunny room that faced the harbor, but the famed Southern California weather had lost its balmy air. Gray clouds scudded across the sky, playing hide-and-seek with the sun. The sea rolled in on dull green waves. Judging by their lacy whitecaps, the breeze from offshore had picked up as well.

Drew chose a table strategically positioned with a view of the stairs, and accepted coffee and juice from the waiter before helping himself to a fresh-baked cranberry muffin from the basket on the table.

He was slathering butter on the hot, fragrant muffin when Tracy appeared.

His first thought was that she should have used a little of the makeup she'd purchased last night. In the harsh light of morning, her face appeared washed-out and the shadows were back under her eyes. She'd caught her rich brown hair back with a scarf, which only emphasized her pallor.

The rest of her looked pretty good, though. Her jeans and scoop-necked navy T-shirt hugged her curves. She'd tied the sleeves of her pea-green windbreaker loosely around her waist. Instead of shielding her hips, the green flap had the paradoxical effect of drawing attention to their trim lines.

The memory of how those hips had butted against his during that wild kiss last night sent a spear of heat through Drew. His fingers tightened on the knife. The muffin came apart in his other hand.

Disgusted, Drew dropped the crumbs onto his plate. When he glanced up again, Tracy had sailed right past the breakfast room and stopped at the front desk.

After a short conversation with the clerk, she accepted the package he retrieved for her and walked out of the inn with a purposeful stride. Muttering a curse, Drew gulped down his coffee and abandoned his muffin.

The salty breeze hit him in the face the moment he exited the inn. Tugging up the zipper of his red jacket with its Classic Motors, Inc. logo, he shoved his hands in the pockets of his jeans and stayed well behind his target as she wound her way down to Crescent Avenue. It was too early for the shops to be open, but the coffee bars and restaurants facing the harbor were doing a brisk business. Tracy ignored them all and made for a golf cart rental stand at the intersection of Crescent and Sumner.

As curious about the package tucked under her arm as her reason for renting wheels so early in the morning, Drew hung back while she completed the necessary rental forms and obtained a map from the agent. After some discussion, the agent used a Magic Marker to outline a route. Moments later she putt-putted out of the lot in a cart painted a bright orange.

As she turned left onto Third Street, Drew strolled into the lot and passed the attendant his driver's license and credit card.

"I'd like to rent a cart."

"That's why we're here. Just sign this release."

Shoving a clipboard across the counter, the clerk processed the credit card while Drew filled out the necessary paperwork and signed the liability release.

"I saw you highlighting a route for the customer who just left," Drew commented. "Is that the best way to see the sights of the island?"

"Sure is. The route takes you along Pebble Beach Road, up into the foothills and back along Avalon Canyon Road to the Wrigley Memorial and Botanical Gardens. Here, I'll mark it for you. Be careful on the turns up in the hills," he warned. "Some of them are pretty sharp."

Drew chose a cart in a more conservative—and less visible—dark green. Tracy was only five minutes ahead when he departed the lot. He wasn't worried about finding her. He'd trailed targets a good deal tougher than Ms. Brandt through the back alleys of Hong Kong and the jungles of Colombia. With only one main route circling the island, Catalina was a piece of cake.

He turned left, then left again to avoid the pedestrians-only portion of Crescent Avenue. Once on Pebble Beach Road he cruised past the ferryboat terminal, a few scattered restaurants and the helicopter port.

Pebble Beach lived up to its name. Driven by the stiff breeze, waves pounded against the stony shoreline. Not a single intrepid bather or sun-worshipper was in sight.

Just past the beach the road curved and inclined sharply. The palms and lush green foliage at shore level gave way to sunbaked foothills dotted with scrub pine and thorny bushes. Another turn led to a steeper incline. Drew put the cart's pedal to the floor but the accelerator had obviously been adjusted to keep tourists from tearing through town. A hungover sea turtle could have passed him as he chugged up the hill.

He gained speed on a level stretch and cruised by a turnout with a spectacular view of the bay. Two steep, zigzagging turns later, he spotted the bright orange cart parked in another turnout, this one at the verge of a steep canyon. The cart's driver sat on the low wall ringing the viewpoint. Hunched over against the wind, she had both arms wrapped around her middle.

Drew cruised to a stop behind her cart. Pasting on his best isn't-this-a-coincidence smile, he cut the engine and swung out. When his target turned to see who had invaded her privacy, Drew's smile disintegrated.

"What's wrong?"

Her eyes were red and swollen. Tears streamed down her cheeks. She swallowed, tried to answer and managed only a small sob.

Drew crouched beside her. "Tracy, talk to me. What's the matter?"

Gulping, she unhunched her shoulders. Only then did he see she held the package the desk clerk had retrieved in her lap.

"I… I promised I'd do it, but…" Her voice was thick with tears. "It's so hard."

"What's hard?"

"Saying goodbye for the last time."

"To what?"

"Not what," she got out, hugging the plastic-wrapped package. "Who."

"Back up a little," Drew said gruffly. "Tell me who you're saying goodbye to."

Her shoulders slumping, she turned her tear-washed eyes to the sea. "My Uncle Jack."

She didn't have an uncle. Not according to Denise. The former Secret Service agent wouldn't miss an entire branch of the Brandt family tree. Drew kept silent, figuring she was using an honorific title to describe the man whose picture she carried in her wallet.

"We weren't actually related," she said after a moment, confirming his guess. "He lived next door to my aunt. He put up a swing for me when I was six or seven and must have fixed my bike a dozen times."

Her hand came up to swipe at her wet cheeks.

"He died a week ago. He'd been sick for a long time. He was ready. I wasn't."

"I'm sorry."

"Me, too," she said with aching regret. "Jack Foster was the only family I had left. Everyone else was gone. My parents. My aunt. I didn't want to let him go. It cost me my job but I had to stay with him until the end. Now… Now I have to fulfill his last wish and scatter his ashes."

Hell, was that what she had in the box she kept clutched to her middle? This Uncle Jack's ashes?

Drew wasn't squeamish. God knew he'd seen his share of corpses. Nor was he particularly sentimental. There wasn't much room for sentiment in his line of work. Yet the realization that Tracy had driven up to this high overlook to perform a final ritual for a man she'd so obviously loved punched a little hole in his heart.

"Why here?" he asked.

"Jack was born and raised in the northwest, but he came here as a young man. He used to take the ferry over whenever his ship was in port. He and his shipmates would dance all night at the Avalon Ballroom."

Sighing, she crossed her arms over the package and drank in the view of clouds scudding across the bay.

"He fell in love here. Very much in love. He told me about it a few days before he died. He was drifting in and out by then. I didn't get the whole story. Only that he left his heart on Catalina all those years ago."

Drew had locked on to the first part of her narrative. Ignoring the rest, he zeroed in on her mention of a ship.

"Was your friend in the navy?"

"The merchant marines. He joined when he was just sixteen and served aboard the USS *Kallister,* home-ported in Long Beach. It was a cargo ship."

"A six-thousand-ton freighter," Drew said grimly, "torpedoed off the coast of California in November 1941—one of the dozen or so U.S. ships that were attacked before we officially entered the war."

Tracy turned a surprised face his way. "I thought vintage cars were your passion. Do you have an interest in old ships, too?"

Damn straight he did. This particular rust bucket, anyway.

"I pulled a hitch in the navy, remember?"

Naively, she accepted that a common sailor would know the tonnage and history of every merchant ship that had ever flown the U.S. flag.

"Sorry, I forgot about that."

"No reason for you to remember it," Drew said, claiming a seat beside her on the low wall. "You've had a lot on your mind lately. Tell me more about Jack."

"He was such a good man. Always willing to lend a helping hand to anyone who needed it. He never married—he used to joke that he was waiting for me to grow up—but now I think he stayed true to this lost love he told me about just before he died."

Drew could care less about the man's love life. He wanted to know more about his ship.

"You said he was based in Long Beach?"

"That's right. It's just a short ferry ride. As I mentioned, he and his shipmates used to come to dances at the Avalon Ballroom whenever their ship was in port. That's why I was so intrigued by Trixie Halston."

Drew's mind immediately clicked on the information Denise had fed him last night about the singer who'd died after a fall from the balcony of the Avalon, but he played dumb to keep Tracy talking.

"Who's Trixie Halston?"

"She was a big band singer. I came across her name when I was searching for information about that song. The one I, uh, told you I heard."

Embarrassment stained her cheeks. Obviously realizing that she must have sounded like a total nutcase yesterday afternoon, she hurried past the awkward incident on the ballroom balcony.

"It's the saddest thing. This singer—Trixie Halston—died here on Catalina. What was even sadder, she died about the time my Uncle Jack left Catalina for the last time. I remember him saying he never came back after the *Kallister* left port but couldn't remember exactly when that was. I Googled up every bit of information I could find about the ship, its history and when it sailed from Long Beach. Unfortunately, I couldn't find much."

Drew regarded her with narrowed eyes. "Let me get this straight. You trolled the Internet looking for information on a ship that left port some time in November *1941?*"

"Yes. Why? Is that so odd?"

Hell, yes, it was odd. Downright eerie, in fact. She obviously didn't know what Drew did—that the same ship had sailed from the same port on the same date some sixty years apart. Skirting her question, he posed one of his own.

"Ever hear the expression 'Loose lips sink ships?' Sailing dates were extremely close hold."

"But this one occurred more than six decades ago! Surely the information is now available to the public."

"It might be," he said carefully, "if the ship in question wasn't still in active service. Even with eyes-in-the-sky satellite technology, we don't publicize sailing dates today any more than we did then."

"So that's why I couldn't find the specific date the *Kallister* left port in 1941. I found plenty of sites that listed the date she was torpedoed, though."

"No surprise there," Drew said dryly. "The enemy would already have that information, so it wasn't necessary to keep it under wraps."

"True. Oh, well, it doesn't really matter. I just got caught up in the juxtaposition of Jack's ship, the haunting tune I heard and the woman who sang it. The puzzle took my mind off what I had to do for a little while."

Gnawing on her lower lip, she glanced down at the package in her lap.

"Guess I'd better get on with it."

Extracting a plain wooden box from its plastic wrapping, she swung her legs over the low wall and walked a little ways away. Drew stayed seated. This was a private ceremony. He wouldn't intrude.

"'Bye, Jack," she murmured, opening the small box. "I'll miss you."

The wind gusted, carrying the ashes across and down the steep hillside. As Drew watched them disperse in a swirl of fine gray dust, he breathed easy for the first time since Lightning had called him in. He could report with ninety-nine percent assurance that Tracy Brandt had no interest in the modern-day *Kallister*'s position and course. That one percent would keep him on her until he was dead certain.

Or *she* was dead.

That possibility morphed into a distinct probability when the wind kicked into a sudden, vicious blast of air.

Tracy's hair tore free of the scarf. The ends lashed into her face. Burdened by the box, she tried to shake the strands back, lost her balance and pitched down the steep canyon slope.

Chapter 5

Tracy tried to stop her fall, but the wind at her back was too strong and the slope too steep.

Tossing the empty box aside, she twisted in mid-air and landed on her hip. The loose rocks propelled her into a bone-jarring slide. Scrabbling for a hand-hold, she grabbed the branch of a prickly juniper. A yelp escaped her as the scaly bark ripped through her palm, taking shreds of skin with it.

Arms and legs flailing, she slid gracelessly down the slope. Stones gouged her back. Brush scraped her cheek. Frantically, she clawed at dirt and rocks and spiny plants until a sudden, torturous yank at her waist almost cut her in half.

"I've got you!"

For the second time in as many days, Drew had grabbed her windbreaker. With the sleeves knotted around her waist, the tough nylon acted like a noose. Tracy couldn't breathe, couldn't move, couldn't do anything except dangle at the end of her tether.

"Can you climb back up?" Drew grunted from above her.

"I... I think so."

She inched her head back, saw his position was almost as precarious as hers. Stretched as taut as a hawser, he held on to her windbreaker with one fist and the spindly trunk of a juniper with the other.

"We'll go slow," he got out, dragging at her dead weight. "Slow and easy."

Tracy took him at his word and crawled up inch by scary inch. Every stone she dislodged and sent rattling into the canyon pared another year off her life. She was into negative numbers by the time she clambered back over the wall and collapsed onto the gravel.

Drew hunkered down beside her. Dirt streaked his chin. The knuckles of one hand were skinned from the diving catch he'd made. Concern carved a deep groove between his eyebrows.

"You hit those rocks hard. Anything broken?"

She waggled both hands and feet. "Everything appears to be in working order." Feeling almost as stupid now as she was shaken, she shoved the hair out of her eyes. "You must think I'm a total klutz."

He answered with a long silence.

"Oh, come on! You can't seriously believe I was trying to take another swan dive."

"What I think," he said slowly, "is that you should see a doctor."

"A psychiatrist, you mean."

"Or a psychologist. I know one. A good one. She—"

"Thank you very much, but I don't need a shrink!"

Ignoring the fact that she herself had begun to wonder if she were losing it, Tracy scrambled to her feet. All she wanted at this point was to put as much space as she could between herself and Andrew McDowell.

What did it matter that his easy smile and sexy bedroom eyes turned her on? So what if the kiss he'd laid on her last night had rocked her off her feet? She didn't have any business getting involved with a man she knew almost nothing about. Particularly one who thought she needed to have her head examined!

What really irritated her was that she'd bared a part of herself to Drew. Told him things she'd never told her callous boss, even when the jerk had made her choose between her job and caring for Jack in his last days. So where did McDowell get off judging her? One kiss didn't give him the keys to her head *or* her heart.

Feeding the flames of a righteous anger mixed with a healthy portion of indignation, she steered her golf cart back down the twisting road. Drew stayed close on her tail. Probably thought she was going to drive off a cliff and into the sea, Tracy fumed.

By the time she putted into town, she'd worked up a full head of steam. She'd turn in the golf cart, she decided. Check out of the inn. Take the ferry back to the mainland and get on with her life. Fired by those intentions, she wheeled through the narrow, one-way streets of Avalon.

She pulled up at a stop sign, fully intending to turn left into the rental lot. Another cart chugged through the intersection. Two tourists strolled the crosswalk.

Tracy followed their progress to the far side of the intersection and caught her breath. There, looming in the distance, was the casino. Its red tile roof was a beacon against the gunmetal gray of the sky.

As if on cue, the melody drifted into her head. She knew it and the lyrics by heart now. She sat for a moment, listening, before giving in to an urge as inexorable and relentless as the pull of the tide. Turning right instead of left, she steered for the casino.

Drew caught up with her on the spit of rock that reached out into the sea. The casino was behind her, the restless, churning sea ahead.

The sun had disappeared behind the wall of gray clouds and the wind was still gusting. It came in off the water in damp, cold blasts, churning the waves into whitecaps and rattling the rigging of the boats anchored in the bay.

Buffeted by the wind and spume, Tracy had pulled on her windbreaker. The hood hid her face until Drew came to stand beside her. When she glanced up to acknowledge his presence, her eyes were bleak.

"Trixie Halston's death wasn't an accident. She was pushed."

Drew leaped to the obvious conclusion. There was only one way this woman could know the details of a sixty-year-old murder.

"Who pushed her? Your Uncle Jack?"

"No! Jack didn't kill her. He wouldn't!"

Almost howling now, the wind snatched his words and seemed to fling them at Tracy. She staggered back a few steps, struggling for breath.

"I think Trixie was the woman he fell in love with. The one whose memory he carried in his heart all these years. He said she was someone special, someone whose star never got to shine."

Drew could hardly hear her. Like a sailor's wife keening over the news of a ship lost at sea, the wind seemed to rage and weep and screech all at the same time. Gritting his teeth, he grasped Tracy's arm.

"Let's go somewhere where we can talk."

Neither the casino nor the small museum at the rear of the building was open yet, but the restaurant next to the museum had raised its shutters. Drew yanked open the door and nudged Tracy inside.

The relief was instant. With the wind shut out and

the welcome scent of fresh-brewed coffee heavy on the air, Drew sent Tracy to claim a table.

"How do you take your coffee?"

"Cream, no sugar."

He joined her a few moments later with two steaming mugs. Except for the woman busy behind the counter, they had the place to themselves. Still, Drew kept his voice low when he picked up where they'd left off.

"You want to tell me how you know this Halston woman was murdered?"

"I don't know *how* I know. I just know."

Well, hell! He'd thought for a moment out there on the rocks that she actually knew what she was talking about.

"Ri-iight," he drawled, leaning back in his chair. "You just know."

The sarcasm brought her chin up. "Let me rephrase that. I *felt* her, Drew. On the ballroom balcony yesterday. Up on the hillside, a while ago. Just now, out on the rocks. I felt her fury and...and her burning desire for revenge. And I hear her despair every time that damned song plays inside my head."

Drew didn't bother to hide his skepticism. Stubbornly, she rushed ahead.

"There's a link," she insisted. "Trixie Halston. Jack. Me. Even you. Something's conspired to pull us together at this time, in this place. You can't deny that."

Something *had* pulled them together. Those

Internet queries she'd zinged off. He wanted to tell her they were what brought him to Catalina, but that niggling one percent doubt kept him silent.

"I don't expect you to believe me," she huffed. "Nor do I expect you to stick around and help me dig in to the facts of Trixie Halston's death. Just don't get in my way. And don't ask questions if all you're going to do is sneer at me when I answer them."

Lightning was going to love this! He'd sent an OMEGA operative to discover the circumstances surrounding Tracy Brandt's sudden interest in a ship carrying a top-secret cargo. Now said operative was apparently going ghost hunting.

What the hell. A few more days with Tracy should resolve the last of Drew's doubts about her. Maybe even present the opportunity for them to lock lips again.

The thought put a kink in his gut. Frowning at his body's involuntary and completely irresponsible reaction to the woman, he laid out a brisk proposal.

"Okay, here's the deal. I'll help you look into this business of Trixie Halston's death. If we find nothing and you're still hearing voices, you get some help."

Drew had already decided that help would come from Claire Cantwell, code name Cyrene. A psychologist by training, she'd become an internationally renowned expert in hostage negotiations after her first husband died at the hands of the thugs who'd kidnapped him for ransom. Now married to her longtime lover, Colonel Luis Esteban, Cyrene was one of OMEGA's most skilled operatives.

"Agreed?"

His steady stare drilled into Tracy. She chewed on the inside of her cheek, considering the offer.

She had to admit this all sounded bizarre, even to her. Yet the rage and despair she'd felt out there on the rocks were so strong. So real.

She could go it alone. Conduct her own research, sift through the few known facts. Unfortunately, her resources were extremely limited. The nasty truth was that she needed Drew's assistance, financially if not emotionally.

"Agreed."

He accepted her capitulation with a nod. "Okay. We'll finish our coffee and get started."

"Started where?"

"I'm thinking the museum next door. My guess is they'll have records of Halston's death since it occurred right here, on their doorstep. Then we'll try the police."

The small museum proved to be a treasure trove of information and artifacts. Sniffing at the rich scents of polished wood, woven baskets and old brass, Tracy and Drew followed a timeline that depicted Catalina's early settlement by Native American tribes some seven thousand years ago to its "discovery" by Spanish explorer Juan Rodriguez Cabrillo in 1542.

Additional exhibits detailed its occupation by Russian otter hunters and its days as a haven for American smugglers before being given as part of a Mexican land grant to Thomas Robbins a few short days before the United States invaded California.

Under U.S. ownership, the island had been used primarily for cattle and sheep ranching, but a growing number of mainlanders sailed across the channel to picnic on the shore and pitch tents in the picturesque coves. By the time the town of Avalon was founded in 1887, Catalina had become a favorite vacation destination.

Tracy found the pictures of the rich and famous who frolicked in Avalon after the turn of the century fascinating, but the big band exhibit riveted her attention. She read every word on every display panel, from the construction of the casino to the first live radio broadcast to the dance marathons and jitterbug contests that drew thousands of Depression-weary participants.

To her disappointment, the exhibit featured the big bands—Harry James, Artie Shaw, Russ Morgan—but not Kenny Jones or his headline singer. Unlike Natalie Wood, whose tragic drowning rated a prominent display, Trixie Halston didn't make the boards. When she and Drew queried the volunteer at the desk, he explained the omission.

"Ms. Halston's death caused a sensation here on the island, of course, but she wasn't a big enough name to generate much publicity outside California. I think our curator has a file on her. I'll ask if you can take a look at it."

"Thanks."

He returned a few moments later with both the file and the curator. A smiling woman in her late thirties, Jane Ireland laid a manila envelope on the counter.

"I understand you're interested in Trixie Halston."

"That's right."

"We don't have much on her. Just this flyer announcing the Jones orchestra's appearance at the ballroom, an autographed publicity shot of the band and a number of newspaper clippings describing Ms. Halston's accident. Oh, and this cassette of her last performance. I had it dubbed from the tape of the live radio broadcast."

Tracy had studied the black-and-white publicity still in the lounge area midway up the ramps to the ballroom. She'd also Googled up the newspaper stories. Drew, on the other hand, was getting his first look at Trixie Halston.

Eyes intent, he studied the woman standing off to the side in the publicity shot. Her padded shoulders, wavy hair and penciled brows were right out of the late '30s. The sultry, come-hither smile was ageless. He searched her heart-shaped face for some signs of the drugs or alcohol Denise had alluded to in her report last night. If Trixie Halston was smoking dope or guzzling gin, they hadn't left their mark on her.

Setting the photo aside, Drew started on the clippings. The hairstyle changed from glossy waves to smooth rolls caught back in what looked like a fishnet. The sharply penciled eyebrows softened. The smile was the same promise of dark, secret delights.

Tearing his gaze from that seductive curve of cheek and lip, Drew skimmed the article. It confirmed what he already knew. Trixie Halston, girl singer with the Kenny Jones Orchestra, plunged to her death from the balcony of the Avalon Casino on the night of November 18th, 1941. Police investigators found no witnesses to the incident and, lacking any evidence to the contrary, the Los Angeles County Coroner ruled her death an accident.

"The LAPD has jurisdiction here on Catalina?" Drew asked the curator.

"They did at that time," she confirmed. "For certain types of cases, anyway. Our chief of police can give the specifics."

"Here's a story about Trixie's funeral," Tracy murmured, smoothing the wrinkles from a yellowed strip of newsprint. "Kenny Jones served as one of the pallbearers. Someone named Ed LaSorta gave the eulogy."

"That's Edward Allen LaSorta, founder and CEO of the LaSorta Agency. He was the orchestra's PR man until it broke up after the war. He started his own firm afterward and did publicity for some big-name stars. From what I hear, he's a force to be reckoned with in Hollywood."

Drew's head came up. "He's still alive?"

"Very much so, although I read somewhere that he's in a wheelchair now."

"How about the band leader, Kenny Jones?"

"He died in the early '50s. I would imagine most of the orchestra members have also passed on. You can probably find a roster of their names on the Internet. I know they recorded a number of albums."

"Mind if we make copies of this article?" Drew asked.

"And the cassette?" Tracy added.

She didn't need a copy. She'd heard Trixie Halston croon via the computer twice now. She could probably pull up more of her recordings. Yet the idea of listening to the singer's very last broadcast sent shivers dancing down her spine.

"I saw an electronics shop on Crescent Avenue, right next to the bakery," Tracy said, cajoling the reluctant curator. "I could make a copy and have this back to you in half an hour."

When Ireland hesitated, a mounting sense of urgency drove Tracy to root around in her purse. She wanted a copy of that tape. She *had* to have it.

Extracting her driver's license and a credit card, she plunked them down on the counter as surety. "Hang on to these until I get back. I won't be more than half an hour, I promise."

She exited the museum with the cassette tucked safely in her pocket. Once outside, Drew suggested a division of labor.

"It's almost ten-thirty. Unless you're planning to stay on the island another night, I suggest you make copies of the tape and the article while I talk to the police chief. If LAPD handled the investigation, I doubt the locals will have much on file but it's worth a shot. I'll meet you back at the inn. We can check out and catch the afternoon ferry back to the mainland. I'm thinking we might want to look up this Ed LaSorta."

"Sounds like a good plan to me."

Tracy was all for catching the afternoon ferry. She'd accomplished what she came here to do and she couldn't really afford another night at the Bella Vista.

Making copies of the newspaper article proved a simple task. Transferring the taped recording to a digital CD proved almost as simple. A helpful clerk inserted the tape into an AM/FM/cassette boom box, plugged its audio-out cable into an audio-in jack on a CD recorder, and hit Play. The high-speed transfer took place with such swift, silent efficiency that the three-hour radio segment went from tape to disk in less than ten minutes.

All Tracy heard was the soft whir of the CD recorder doing its thing. Disappointed, she bit back the urge to ask the clerk to replay it. She still had to return the cassette and hustle back to the inn to pack. She'd have to wait to listen to her personal copy of the recording.

"Here you are, ma'am."

"Thanks. How much do I owe you?"

"No charge. We get blank promo CDs by the bucketful. Just come back and see us when you're in the market for a new TV or MP3 player."

She didn't have the heart to tell him TVs and MP3 players weren't anywhere on her radar screen at the moment. Tucking the CD in her purse, she hurried out of the shop and winced when her elbow bumped the door. Evidently she'd collected a few bruises during her slide down the rocky slope. She suspected she'd feel them tomorrow.

A half hour later Drew rapped on her door at the inn to tell her he'd come up empty at the police station. The current chief hadn't been born when Trixie Halston died.

"His files confirmed that LAPD detectives investigated the case and collected evidence," Drew told her. "I've got some contacts in L.A. I'll ask them to see what they can dig up. You packed and ready to go?"

Tracy threw a glance around the cozy room. Her stay on Catalina had been short and eventful, to say the least. She was ready to hop on the ferry and put the island behind her. Yet she couldn't shake the most ridiculous sense of loss, as if she were abandoning a part of herself.

"I'm all packed. I'll meet you down in the lobby."

"It won't take me long to throw my things together." Drew checked his watch. "The next ferry leaves at 12:45. We can make that one if we grab lunch at the pier."

The sky was still overcast when the hovercraft pulled away from the pier. Despite the sharp bite to the air, Tracy stood at the rail, her hair whipping wildly, until the ferry rounded the northern tip of the island and the Avalon Casino disappeared from view.

Chapter 6

Drew had a rental car parked at the ferry terminal in Dana Point. Tracy should have guessed a man who made his living restoring classic cars wouldn't rent a sedate sedan. His vehicle of choice was a low-slung, high-powered Mustang convertible in Torch Red.

Grimacing, she contorted her now aching muscles into the passenger seat. Drew tossed their bags in the trunk and got behind the wheel without displaying the least hint of stiffness. Either he was in much better shape than she was or he made a habit of stretching every sinew and tendon in his body to keep klutzy females from tumbling down canyons. Tracy figured the correct answer was probably *A*.

"I asked my contacts in L.A. to track down this Edward LaSorta," he said after he'd pulled out of the parking lot and started north on Route 1. "They should have something for me by the time we hit the city. If LaSorta's available, we might be able to get in to see him late this afternoon. If not," he added, "my company keeps a condo in the city. We can stay there for as long as it takes to run down these leads."

Tracy shifted uncomfortably in her seat. Her limited finances were one of the primary reasons she'd agreed to include Drew McDowell in this odd quest. He didn't appear to have any qualms about expending time and money in the search for answers about Trixie Halston. Still, she had to quash a nasty little niggle of guilt over allowing to him finance the entire operation.

"I don't want to impose on you or your company."

"Not a problem. Charlie and I do a lot of business out here on the coast. Maintaining a base of operations is more convenient than working out of hotels."

Tracy hadn't realized restoring vintage automobiles was such a profitable enterprise. Drew and his ex-father-in-law must do very well indeed to warrant a condo in L.A.

He didn't look like a high roller, she thought with a quick, sideways glance. He wasn't into flashy rings or gold chains. His jeans and the faded denim shirt he wore under his red windbreaker didn't sport any designer labels. His watch had a plain black leather strap, although its chrome face and complicated array of dials indicated he probably hadn't purchased it at a local discount store.

Yet everything about him hinted at power, if not wealth. She'd met few men as coolly self-confident. Fewer still with such a hard, muscled body.

Last night had given her a feel for just *how* hard and muscled it was. Tracy still didn't understand how she'd ended up in Drew's arms, but she couldn't deny the brief contact had left its mark. She'd tossed and turned afterward, scorched by the searing pleasure he'd generated with his hands and mouth. She'd never burned so hot, so fast for any man.

Not that she'd had all that many incendiary experiences. She'd dated her share in high school and college and enjoyed a couple of semi-serious relationships since. The most recent had fizzled a few months ago, when Jack's increasing illness had demanded all Tracy's time and energy. None of those men had burst into her life with the same intensity as Drew McDowell, however. Certainly none had ever made her forget who or where she was.

Now Drew had dangled the tantalizing possibility of sharing a condo with her. Tracy couldn't help wondering if he expected to pick up where they'd left off last night. The sixty-four-thousand-dollar question was whether she wanted him to.

The sudden quivering low in her belly provided one response, common sense another. The two of them would go their separate ways after L.A. She'd probably never see him again. Plus, he'd offered to refer her to a shrink. She'd be a fool to hop in the sack with someone who thought she had a screw loose.

On the other hand...

The man was most definitely stud material. Why not let nature take its course? What would be the harm if they indulged in an uncomplicated, no-strings-attached tussle between the sheets?

Drew's cell phone interrupted her internal debate. Managing the leather-wrapped wheel easily with one hand, he flipped open the razor-thin phone with the other.

"McDowell here."

He kept his eyes on the road during the short, one-sided conversation. When he flipped the phone shut, he gave Tracy the news.

"Ed LaSorta is in town, but unavailable until tomorrow. We have an appointment with him at his office at eleven a.m. We'll swing by and talk to the detective who's digging in to the Halston case file for us after we meet with LaSorta."

"Your contacts are certainly efficient."

"Yes, they are."

"So we have nothing on the agenda for the rest of today?"

"Just as well. We won't hit L.A. until close to four. Depending on rush-hour traffic, it could take another hour or more to make it to the condo."

Skillfully steering the Mustang around a lumbering semi, he offered a casual suggestion.

"What do you say to just taking it easy this evening? I could use a decent dinner after the fish taco we grabbed at the ferry terminal. There's a Nick's Steakhouse not far from the condo."

Tracy's belly quivered again. She'd kill for a leisurely dinner at one of the elegant establishments owned by the internationally renowned restaurateur, Nick Jensen. The mere idea of sitting across from Drew, sipping a fine Merlot and feasting on beef tournedos cooked in a rich porcini mushroom sauce produced hot licks of anticipation.

Unfortunately, it also produced another rush of guilt. Much as she wanted to, she couldn't keep mooching off this man.

"I have to be honest with you, Drew. I'm counting pennies while I'm between jobs. I can't afford dinner at a high-priced restaurant."

"You can afford this one. There won't be a tab."

"Why not?"

A small smile played at the corners of his mouth. "I do business with the owner."

She made a last, valiant attempt. "All I have with me are a clean pair of slacks and a sweater. I'm not sure they're appropriate for a classy place like Nick's."

"This is Southern California. Nick's patrons will be decked out in everything from nose rings to diamond-studded flip-flops. Slacks and a sweater will be fine."

* * *

Route 1 followed the coast, providing intermittent views of the sea while winding through trendy resort towns. As the Mustang approached the outskirts of L.A., the urban sprawl grew denser and the glimpses of the ocean less frequent.

Drew obviously knew his way around the metropolis. He negotiated the network of intersecting freeways with assurance and appeared unperturbed by the rush-hour traffic that clogged all eight lanes of I-405. By contrast, Tracy was feeling frayed around the edges by the time they pulled into the underground parking lot of a high-rise condo in Marina Del Ray.

She couldn't blame her frazzled nerves entirely on the bumper-to-bumper traffic. The prospect of a whole evening in Drew's company had renewed the fierce debate she'd conducted with herself earlier.

Would he try to pick up where they'd left off last night, or wouldn't he?

Should she encourage him if he did, or shouldn't she?

When an elevator whisked them up twelve stories and Drew escorted her into a two-bedroom unit with a spectacular view of the marina and the Pacific beyond, Tracy was no closer to resolving the debate than she'd been on the road.

"I'll call Nick's to reserve a table," Drew said, depositing her small roll-on on a bench in a bedroom

almost as large as her entire Puget Sound apartment. "Seven o'clock okay?"

"Seven's fine."

"Good. That'll give us time to have a drink and watch the sunset. The show can be pretty awesome with a cloud cover like this."

He hadn't exaggerated, Tracy discovered after she'd changed into her clean slacks and fluffy green sweater and joined him in the living room.

The room was furnished with a gray suede sectional sofa and a matching, man-size easy chair. Floor-to-ceiling glass windows gave a panoramic view of the marina and the spectacle beyond it. As the sun sank toward the Pacific, brilliant rays illuminated the dark clouds from the bottom up. Tinted to gold at their base, they drifted above a sea burnished the same glorious gilt.

"We get similar sunsets on the Washington coast," she murmured, dropping onto the L-shaped sofa, "but nothing quite as dramatic as this."

"I think the smog defuses the city's lights, which in turn intensifies the offshore effect. I poured you a scotch. Neat. No sense watering down good hooch." Grinning, he clinked his tumbler against the one he handed her. "Here's to you and here's to me."

Too polite to tell her host that she'd prefer wine, Tracy took a cautious taste. The scotch had a smooth, smoky bite—unlike Jack's favorite whiskey, which had watered her eyes. Hiding her distaste, she'd sipped at it on more than one occasion to keep him company.

A familiar pain spread through her at the memory. She wouldn't share any more of what he'd insisted were medicinal nips with him. Or exchange idle conversation while they waited to see yet another of his many doctors. Or hold back tears while he struggled for every wheezing breath.

Jack was gone. She'd lost him once in the hospice, again this morning when she'd scattered his ashes. All Tracy had left of him were memories and the puzzle of his link to a big band singer. With a jolt, she remembered the CD tucked inside her purse.

"We've still got some time," she said to Drew. "If you have a CD player, we could listen to Trixie Halston's last broadcast."

He gestured toward the bank of cabinets taking up the opposite wall. "The entertainment center plays everything but five card stud."

"I'll get the CD."

Afterward Drew could never pinpoint exactly when he lost control of the evening. All he could say with any certainty was that it happened sometime during Trixie Halston's opening number.

She didn't come on right away. The broadcast kicked off with the wail of a muted cornet. A few bars later, a full orchestra broke into a fast-paced swing tune Drew didn't recognize. As the introductory song swelled to a finish, applause thundered through the speakers and the bandleader boomed into the mike.

"Hello, all you jive cats and alligators. This is Kenny Jones, coming to you from the beautiful Avalon Ballroom. With me is my orchestra, featuring Tom Delaney on the skins…"

He paused for a drumroll.

"Hal Purdue with his gob stick…"

The trill of a clarinet soared through the night.

"The one, the only Gus Rosendorf on the tin horn."

The cornet was unmuted this time, its notes as pure as liquid silver.

"And with us tonight, as she is every night on the road, is our incomparable canary, Trixie Halston."

Drew's gut tightened in anticipation, but the singer didn't take the mike. He imagined her stepping forward to wave to the two thousand or so couples on the ballroom's enormous dance floor before resuming her seat at the side of the stage.

The bands were the draw back then, the singers merely adjuncts. Big names like Frank Sinatra, Dinah Shore and Jo Stafford had begun their careers by crooning just a few stanzas at a time, and then only when the song called for vocal accompaniment.

"We'll be swinging out for your listening and dancing pleasure until the wee small hours of the morning," Jones announced to the backdrop of a slower tune. "So get ready to give it a ride and go to town."

Tracy rested her head against the back of the sofa.

Her gaze was on the lights coming to life in the marina, but Drew could tell the scene wasn't registering. She balanced her tumbler of scotch on the sofa arm. Her nails tapped the rhythm against the heavy crystal.

"Nice tune," he commented. "What is it?"

"'Blue Orchids.' Hoagy Carmichael's number-one hit in 1939."

Drew was impressed. Her research rivaled Denise's, and she hadn't had OMEGA's considerable resources to tap into. When the song swirled to a finish, she blew out a breath and tipped up her glass.

"Ready for a refill?"

She glanced down, surprised to find the tumbler empty, and shrugged. "Sure. Why not?"

He went easier on the second round. Neither of them had eaten breakfast. Lunch was a tuna taco scarfed down on the ferry. He could hold his scotch on an almost empty stomach, but Tracy already seemed to be loosening up.

She was on her feet now, moving to the beat of another song. "I love this one. 'I'm Nobody's Baby.' Les Santly and Milt Ager hit the charts with it, but Kenny gives it a real west coast swing."

She took the glass Drew handed her, downed a long swallow and set the scotch on the coffee table. Eyes closed, she dipped her shoulders from side to side. Her palms patted her thighs in time to the lively beat. Her dark hair brushed the shoulders of her V-neck sweater. When she began to hum, Drew tried to figure out how the air had taken on such a high voltage. The hair on his forearms was standing at attention.

Suddenly Tracy's eyes flew open. Excitement shimmered in their green depths. "Here comes the vocal."

The singer was indisputably Trixie Halston. Although Drew had heard her croon only a few bars via his cell phone last night, her smoky contralto and satin-sheets delivery had made an indelible impression. They hit even harder when magnified by high-watt speakers.

Christ, she knew how to sell a song! Toying with the tempo, she punched up the lyrics at unexpected points and made the melody her own. Drew had no idea how she managed to block out thousands of feet shuffling across a parquet dance floor, but she did. In the process she conveyed the impression that she was delivering the song directly to him. By the end of the first stanza, he was semihard.

A few seconds later, Tracy took him to fully erect. Laying a hand against the base of her throat, she joined Halston for the second stanza. Their voices melded so perfectly Drew couldn't tell the professional from the amateur. Spellbound, he set down his drink and leaned an elbow on the back of a chair to enjoy the duet.

The vocal ended. The orchestra wrapped the final refrain. Psyched by her performance, Tracy whirled in a circle.

"Didn't that put you in the groove?"

What it had put him in was a sweat.

"The band's still frisking their whiskers," she said with a dreamy smile. "They'll quit mugging light and riff it in the next set."

Whatever the hell that meant. Trying to decipher her odd phrasing, he shot her a curious look. "How did you learn so much about the swing era?"

She didn't hear him. Head cocked, she'd picked up the introductory bars of the next song. Her mouth twisted into a grimace.

"'Careless.'"

"Who is?"

"The song." She flapped a hand toward the entertainment center. "That's 'Careless,' one of Eddie Howard's lollypop hits. Too slow and sweet for my taste, but smooth as a baby's butt."

Drifting on the liquid notes, she glided across the carpet. "Dance with me."

All the reasons he should claim two left feet and take a pass jumped instantly into Drew's head. Although he'd pretty much absolved Tracy of deliberate intent to ferret out classified information about the *Kallister*, he knew damned well she was vulnerable right now. Grieving for a man she'd loved and cared for in his final days. Caught up to the point of obsession in a mystery from the past. Uncertain about her future. He'd be ten kinds of a jerk to take advantage of that vulnerability.

"C'mon, Drew." Her hands flattened against his shirtfront. Her body swayed into his. "Dance with me."

The contact ignited an instant heat. Fully aware he was playing with matches, he slid an arm around her waist and brought her against him.

Drew didn't consider himself much of a hoofer. Nor had he indulged in the recent craze for ballroom dancing. His closest encounter had come when he'd flipped on the TV and caught a few seconds of *Dancing with the Stars* before switching to a pro basketball game. But the beat was slow and Tracy matched her moves to his with a skill that made him feel like he'd just aced Arthur Murray 101.

The decorator who'd outfitted the condo had strategically positioned area rugs to soften the hardwood flooring. The two-inch-thick Flokati in the living room forced Drew to keep a wary eye on his direction as he navigated toward an open stretch. Once clear of all potential hazards, his partner claimed his full and undivided attention.

"It's been so long since I got out on a dance floor," she murmured, snuggling her cheek against his shoulder. "This feels so good."

Good wasn't the adjective he would have used. In a few slow turns, she'd wound him tighter than the rocker arm of a '64 T-bird. The top of her head rested just under his chin. Her breasts were mounded against his chest. Drew could feel their soft, sensual press with every breath she took.

He tucked her closer, cradling her hips and thighs. He kept his moves timed to the song, but his pulse revved and his blood raced. There was no way he could hide her effect on his body.

When her hip bumped against his, he fully expected her to end the dance at that point. Or at least put a few inches of air between them. Instead, she lifted her head and curved her mouth in a teasing smile.

"It's been a long time since I felt *that,* too."

Last night Drew had badly misread her signals. This one came through loud and clear. Still, he'd learned to take nothing for granted with this woman.

"If you want me to back off," he warned in a low growl, "now's the time to say so."

The teasing light left her eyes. Pursing her lips in an invitation as provocative as it was unmistakable, she slid her arms around his neck.

"The last thing I want you to do right now is back off."

Drew didn't need a second invitation. His heart slamming against his ribs, he covered her mouth with his. She welcomed the rough kiss with a hunger that jacked his temperature up another ten degrees. Teeth scraping, tongues mating, they remained locked together until tasting and touching wasn't enough for either of them.

The last of Drew's control was fast slipping its leash when Tracy jerked back. Her cheeks flushed, her mouth red and wet from his kiss, she angled her head.

"Listen!"

He recognized the tune in the first few bars. "I'll Walk Alone" was Trixie Halston's signature song, the one she'd recorded as a single.

Drawn like a moth to a flame, Tracy eased out of his hold and drifted toward the speakers. She hummed the instrumental portion of the song, then joined Trixie in a promise to wait, to hoard her smiles and her laughter, until she could give them to the one she loved. When the song ended, tears trailed glistening tracks down her cheeks.

Enough was enough, Drew decided. She didn't need this kind of emotional turmoil. Switching off the stereo, he moved to her side and slid a comforting hand under the silky mass of her hair.

"Are you okay?"

She lifted her eyes to his. The naked pain in them knifed right through him.

"Isn't it ironic?" she got out, her voice ragged.

"What?"

"That song. It became both a hit and an epitaph."

"I guess it did."

A shudder ripped through her. Swiping at her tears, she lifted her chin and forced a brittle laugh.

"Enough with the sourpusses! We need food. Lights. Laughter. Let me fix my face and we'll blow this joint."

If he'd needed a reminder of her volatile mood swings, she'd just delivered one. In the blink of an eye, she'd morphed from tragic to tinsel-bright. She started for the bedroom, calling a request over her shoulder as she went.

"Be a sweetie and top off my scotch. I could use a stiff belt while I repair the damages."

Christ! She didn't even *sound* like the same woman. Frowning, Drew retrieved her glass, but left his own untouched. The eighteen-year-old Glenlivet delivered a kick. He knew his limits.

"Here you are."

Tracy was at the lighted dressing table in the guest bedroom. She hadn't wasted any time emptying the entire contents of her cosmetics bag onto the table. Brushes, tubes and plastic cases littered the marbled surface. Perched on a round swivel stool, she swiped at her lashes with a mascara wand and smiled at him in the mirror.

"Thanks."

With a word of caution, he started out. "You haven't eaten much today, Tracy. You might want to go easy on that."

"Tracy?" She gave a disdainful snort. "That powder puff couldn't carry her liquor in a milk pail."

Drew stopped. Turned. Stared at the brunette busily darkening her lashes.

"What did you say?"

"You heard me." Scrunching one eye shut, she started on the other. "She's a sweet patootie, our little Miss Tracy, but one drink gets her half ossified."

Drew went still.

The woman seated before the mirror glanced up, noted his frozen immobility and flashed him a grin.

"I know! I almost blew my wig the first time it happened, too."

"The first time *what* happened?" he asked carefully.

"This! Me!" Kicking with one foot, she twirled the stool in a full circle. "It comes and goes. I don't know how or why. But I'm here now, baby. Trixie's here."

Chapter 7

Dread crawled up Drew's spine, inch by cold inch. Tracy had flipped out. Lost it completely. And he'd helped push her over the edge.

He should never have played along with her. Never have agreed to search for information regarding Trixie Halston's death. All he'd done was feed her obsession with the dead singer until she could no longer distinguish fantasy from reality.

"Tracy, listen to me. We need to—"

"Tracy's not here. It's me, Drew. Trixie. Awww, you don't believe me. I'm not surprised."

Abandoning the stool, she approached him. A bright, almost feverish excitement lit her eyes.

"I think it was the music that brought me out. Or the dancing. You sure know how to cut a rug, by the way."

"Jesus, Tracy!"

"I keep telling you, she's not here."

As she had when she'd begged him to dance with her, she laid her palms on his chest. His muscles jumped at the touch. Smiling like a cat at his reaction, she purred up at him.

"I could show you a good time, baby. Much better than that little Minnie."

Drew stared down at her flushed face and over-bright eyes and wanted to kick himself. Hell! He should have spotted the signs before. She must have snorted something stronger than scotch. He hadn't found any trace of drugs when he'd searched her room last night, but the woman was flying high.

If she were a user, that could account for her financial dilemma. It could also explain her interest in the *Kallister*, Drew realized, his jaw locking. She needed money to feed her habit. Maybe she thought she could get it by selling classified information.

His doubts resurfacing like obnoxious, uninvited guests, he decided he had only one option at this point. He'd play along with her until he could search her things again. In the meantime, he'd get on the horn to Denise and ask her to have Claire Cantwell jump the first plane out.

"Whoever you are," he drawled to the woman

who'd once again become his target, "you need to eat. So do I. Why don't we continue this conversation over a steak?"

"I'll be ready in two blinks of your peepers."

Nick Jensen took the call from OMEGA's control center while driving home from a dinner at the White House. His wife sat beside him, still pumped from sharing a table with the Swedish ambassador and her escort—who just happened to head one of Sweden's largest electronics firms. While everyone else at the table talked politics, Mackenzie had drilled the engineer for details about his company's breakthrough application of millimeter-wave, high-linearity technology.

Nick had learned to live with his wife's fascination for all things electronic. Formerly his chief of communications, she now headed a special, super high-tech unit that supported OMEGA and several other agencies.

Unfortunately, *she* hadn't learned to leave her work at the office. Their centuries-old town house in Alexandria bristled with every wireless device sold on the open market and a good number that hadn't yet made it into commercial applications. Despite instincts honed to a razor's edge by the years he'd spent in the field before taking over as director of OMEGA, Nick regularly tripped some silent switch or another. The last time he'd shattered three windows before figuring out how to turn the ear-blasting volume on her megadecibel MP3 player down instead of up.

Grimacing at the memory, he responded to the discreet buzz of his phone. After a quick glance at the digital display, he flipped up the lid and aimed the built-in camera at his right eye.

"This is Lightning."

OMEGA's scramblers decoded his encrypted signal with real-time efficiency. Denise Kowalski's brisk voice answered.

"Hi, Chief. GPS indicates you've left the White House."

"Roger that. Mac and I are on our way home. What's up?"

"I just got an interesting report from Riever, along with a request for backup. Seems Tracy Brandt has either flipped out or shot up. She thinks she's a ghost."

"Did you just say ghost?"

"Affirmative. Want me to give you the details now or wait until you get home?"

"We'll swing by the control center. You can brief us there."

With a slither of her satin-lined evening cape, Mackenzie popped up in her seat. "What's this about a ghost?"

"Drew just called in. His target claims she is one."

"You're kidding."

"I wish I were," Nick said grimly, his mind on the cargo aboard the USS *Kallister*. The possibility that someone as unstable as this Tracy Brandt apparently was might have dug up information concerning the super-secret munitions put a kink in his gut.

"Riever's requesting backup," he told his wife.

"What does he want? A shrink or a team of ghost busters?"

"We'll find out when we get to the control center."

Nick checked the rearview mirror and swung the wheel of his 1951 Bugatti in a sharp right turn. Drew had hunted down and restored the Bugatti for him just last year. The gleaming maroon roadster represented the curious twists Nick's life had taken. Born and raised in the back alleys of Cannes before being adopted by Doc Jensen, another former OMEGA agent, Nick got a kick out of wheeling around D.C. in a vehicle manufactured by the French firm that had dominated the racing circuit for decades.

Short minutes later he turned onto the street that led to OMEGA's underground parking. Reinforced titanium doors shielded the facility's entrance. Nick buzzed Denise, who activated the doors. Parking the Bugatti in his reserved space, Nick rounded the roadster's trunk to assist his wife. Her gown of shimmering silver showed off her slender figure to perfection, but made exiting the low-slung sports car something of a challenge.

Once granted entry to the third-floor control center, Mackenzie tossed aside her cape and greeted Denise with the easy familiarity of old friends.

Although they'd grown close over the years, the two were as different as women in the same profession could be. Sandy-haired Denise approached her responsibilities with dead seriousness and rarely cracked a smile. Her husband, Hank McGowan, ascribed that bone-deep sense of duty to her years with the Secret Service. Unlike other law enforcement officials, Secret Service agents were trained to jump into, not away from, the line of fire. Few of them joked about their work.

By contrast, Mackenzie had a quicksilver smile and an excess of energy that made it hard for her to sit still. Perching on the edge of the controller's console, she swung a foot encased in a sparkly silver mule.

"I can't wait to hear this! How did Riever wind up with a poltergeist?"

"He says the target is so fixated on this Trixie Halston that she's lost her grip on reality. She thinks she *is* the dead singer."

"When did she come to that conclusion?" Nick asked.

"Tonight, apparently, although Riever says she's shown evidence of an obsessive fixation prior to this. Supposedly she's adopted odd speech patterns and uses slang right out of the thirties and forties. Phrases like…"

Ever precise, Denise reached for her handwritten log and consulted her notes.

"Hooch, in the groove, and cut a rug."

"What does that last one mean?" Mackenzie wanted to know.

"I had to look it up to be sure. It's derived from the term used to describe heavy foot traffic on a section carpet, causing it to show more wear than the rest. The phrase evolved into slang for dancing in the twenties."

"Hey, she's speaking speakeasy."

Nick winced at his wife's outrageous pun. "What kind of backup does Riever want?"

"He's requested we send Cyrene. I've got her on standby, waiting for the go-ahead from you. He's also requested a technical crew," she added with a glance at Mackenzie.

OMEGA's guru of gadgets and spy-ware perked up. "What does Riev want from us?"

"Evidently the target claims the ghost comes and goes. Riever says he's seen some evidence of that in changes in Brandt's behavior and physical appearance. He wants us to document both."

"My guys are gonna love this!" Mackenzie hooted gleefully. "We've done surveillance on everyone from the mistress of an oil magnate to a homicidal Nobel Prize winner. This will be our first ghost."

"When can Cyrene go into the field?" Nick asked.

"She said Luis had to fly down to Mexico for the week. She can reschedule her appointments and hop a plane as soon as you give the word."

"Send her." He checked his watch, saw it was only

a little after 8:00 p.m. west coast time. "What's Riever doing now?"

"Wining and dining at Nick's L.A."

"Good choice," Lightning commented with a smile.

His restaurants were favorite watering holes for the rich and famous. As a consequence, he employed a *very* high-priced security director to ensure some crazed stalker or hired hitman didn't take out a guest in the middle of dessert. Every one of his restaurants was equipped with a surveillance system so sophisticated it had earned even his wife's approval.

"I'll call my director of security and have him train the cameras on Riever's booth. I want to see what he's dealing with."

"You mean *who* he's dealing with," Mackenzie quipped. "Tracy Brandt or Trixie Halston."

For all the enjoyment Drew derived from his meal, he might just as well have ordered chopped sirloin instead of the succulent and outrageously expensive chateaubriand-for-two he shared with Tracy.

Or Trixie, as she kept insisting he call her.

His head told him this was the same woman who'd munched contentedly on fish and chips on Catalina's Green Pier yesterday. The same heartbroken mourner who'd bid a tearful goodbye to a man she so obviously loved only this morning.

Yet everything about her seemed so damned different. Her hair, her makeup, her speech. As if she *had* slipped into the skin of a singer used to taking center stage and performing for an audience.

She was certainly at the top of her form now. Her low, sexy laugh turned the heads of every male at the surrounding tables. The way she leaned her elbows on the linen tablecloth, dipping the V of her sweater provocatively, brought the waiters back with a prompt efficiency impressive even for Nick's. Despite the attention, she appeared oblivious to every man in the restaurant except Drew. Her focus stayed fixed on him, projecting the fantasy that he formed the center of her universe, that he was the only male in the room.

Like Trixie Halston, when she stepped up to a mike.

The comparison sent a chill down Drew's backbone. Letting his fork clatter onto his gold-rimmed china plate, he shoved both to the side. His dinner companion observed the move with a lift of one eyebrow.

"You've barely touched your steak. I thought you were hungry."

"I thought I was, too. Listen, Tracy, we need to talk about what happened back there at the condo."

"Trixie," she corrected with exaggerated patience. "As for what happened at the condo…"

Leaning forward, she propped her chin in one hand. Drew's gaze zinged to the valley between her breasts. A moment later, her stockinged foot worked its way inside his pants leg and stroked his calf.

Grinning at his carefully neutral expression, she dropped her voice to a murmur.

"I'm looking forward to a repeat performance."

Drew couldn't say the same at the moment. He thought he'd been lusting after Tracy Brandt. Now he wasn't sure who the hell he'd taken in his arms.

"I'm talking about this business of you being Trixie Halston reincarnated. Where's that coming from?"

"I don't know." Her shoulders lifted in a careless shrug. "It just…happens."

"What's the trigger? Booze? Drugs? Sexual stimulation?"

He watched her closely, but saw only confusion and a touch of impatience in her face.

"I told you. I don't know. What does it matter? I'm here. For now, anyway. Serves her right, too."

"Who?"

"Prissy little Tracy Brandt." Her mouth hardened into a thin, crimson line. "You saw her this morning. Crying and carrying on over the bastard who shoved me off that balcony."

A blast of cold air cut through the booth, rattling the silverware. Its icy chill matched the coldness that coated Drew's veins. So he'd guessed right. Tracy knew Trixie Halston had been murdered because she'd spent weeks caring for the man who killed her.

Tracy said Jack had been going in and out during his last days. The secret he'd carried for so many years must have slipped out. Or maybe he confessed, hoping to ease his conscience at the end. A shock like that could throw someone who looked on him as a warm, loving stand-in grandfather completely off-kilter. Shatter her grip on reality. Make her go to the extreme of assuming the victim's identity to atone for Jack's sins.

Wishing like hell Cyrene were here to process all this, Drew continued to probe. "Are you saying your Uncle Jack murdered Trixie Halston?"

Silverware rattled again. The wine goblets rocked on their tall stems.

"Yes," she hissed. "Jack killed me. Only he wasn't my uncle. He was my lover. And he went by John back then. Johnny." Pain and fury warred in her face. "I still can't believe he pushed me onto those rocks."

"Why did he do it?"

"I don't know! He'd asked me to marry him. I put him off. I had a career. I was going places. But the rumors started circulating that he was shipping out. I was afraid I'd never see him again. So I sent him a note and asked him to meet me after the last set. Then…then…"

Her hands curled into fists. Rage edged out all trace of pain.

"Then he snuck up on me. Didn't even have the courage to look me in the face. Just came out of the dark and planted his fist between my shoulder blades."

"If he came at you from behind, how do you know it was him?"

"Who else could it have been! I'd left him an urgent message. Told him to meet me on the balcony. I saw him come into the ballroom, then lost him in the crowd. He was waiting for me, out there in the darkness."

The air around her seemed to crackle. Her fury was like a living thing.

"Now he'd dead, too. I wanted to smash something when Little Miss Tracy sobbed over him this morning. The way she spread his ashes so reverently, you'd think they were the Holy Grail or something. The whole, pitiful act made me want to shove *her* off a balcony."

Her eyes glittered. Her lips curled.

"Or off a cliff."

Drew reacted instinctively. Shooting out his arm, he caught her wrist. "That's enough."

Her furious gaze flew from his face to the hand banding her wrist. When she tried to yank free, he pinned her forearm to the table and issued a soft warning.

"You've passed the point of being entertaining, Tracy."

"Trixie, dammit! Trixie!"

She made another attempt to free herself. Drew tightened his grip. Their brief struggle seemed to burn the last of her energy. With a muttered curse, she slumped back in her chair. Her breath escaped on a shuddering sigh.

Bit by bit the air around them lost its violent feel.

When Drew released her, she sat in silence for a few moments before dragging her napkin from her lap.

"I'm not hungry anymore, either. Can we leave?"

Chapter 8

The occupants of the Mustang made the short drive back to the condo wrapped in tense silence. Tracy kept her hands buried in her lap, trying without success to still their tremors.

The violence at the restaurant had shaken her to her core. She knew she'd exploded in a furious burst of energy. Knew she'd been swept up in a vortex of rage and pain and unbearable heartache. She'd heard the accusations spew out of her mouth. Horrified, she'd tried to stem the vicious tide, but the hurt boiling inside her was too great, the fury too fierce. The realization that she hadn't been able to halt the flow was as terrifying as the growing sense that Trixie Halston hated *her* almost as much as she did Jack.

"He didn't kill you," she whispered fiercely to the woman whose spirit had violated her mind and her body. "I know he didn't!"

Drew cut her a sharp glance. In the intermittent wash of passing headlights, his face was taut, his jaw set.

"Tracy?"

She shifted sideways. The seat belt bit into her shoulder. "Don't believe what you heard back there at the restaurant. Those awful things I said weren't true! None of them! Jack Foster didn't kill Trixie Halston. He didn't have an evil bone in his body!"

Drew's knuckles showed white on the leather-wrapped steering wheel. He speared her with another hard look.

"So that was you saying those things? You, not Trixie?"

She dug her nails into her palms. How could she explain to him what she herself could barely comprehend?

"We were both there. I could feel her rage and despair. I could hear her saying those awful things. But I couldn't stop her, Drew. I couldn't stop her!"

The spiraling panic in her voice warned Tracy she was close to the edge. It must have sent the same signal to Drew. Reining in what she knew had to be a scorching disbelief, he tempered his tone.

"I made some calls before we left for dinner. That

friend I told you about? The psychologist? She's willing to fly out here and talk to you."

Unclenching her fists, Tracy scrubbed the heel of one hand against her left temple. She needed professional help. She accepted that now. This business with Trixie Halston was tearing her apart. Unfortunately, real life played havoc with her visitor from the afterlife.

"I'll talk to someone when I get home," she said dully. "I can't afford to pay travel expenses as well as a consulting fee."

"Claire's doing this as a favor to me."

The flat statement didn't invite further discussion or debate. Just as well, since Tracy was too drained to argue. She was also more than a little frightened. The malevolence she'd heard coming out of her own mouth had scared the crap out of her.

The Marina Del Ray high-rise condominium appeared like a beacon in the night. Drew wheeled past the tall, illuminated palms fringing the property and pulled into the underground parking. He and Tracy had said little in the elevator that whisked them up to the twelfth floor. Once inside the condo, however, he tossed the car keys onto the credenza and demanded clarification on a point that had been bugging him for the past hour or so.

"You said you and Trixie were both there, at the

restaurant. What about here? Before we left for
Nick's? Was that you in my arms? Or her?"

"Me. Mostly. I think." Forehead scrunched, she
thought about it for a moment. "No, I'm sure. That
was pretty much all me."

His skeptical silence provoked a blunt admission.

"Okay, I don't usually come on so strong or force
reluctant males to dance with me. I guess I was
feeling a little raw after everything that's happened
in the past few days. The music got to me. Or the
scotch," she added with a wry grimace. "Believe it
or not, I don't usually drink like a sailor, either."

When Drew declined to comment on that, she
tossed the ball back in his court.

"All right, let's turn this around. Who do *you* think
you held in your arms?"

"You, Tracy. Only you. And to keep the record
straight, I wasn't unwilling. Just the opposite, in fact."

The delicate pink that colored her cheeks told him
she hadn't forgotten the contact between her hip and
the hard bulge behind his zipper.

"Oh. Well. Okay, then. We both agree. That was
me you locked lips with."

Hunching her shoulders, she crossed her arms
around her middle. The neck of her sweater gaped.
Drew knew damned well the resulting display of
cleavage was unintentional. This time. That didn't
make it any easier to wrench his gaze from the
creamy swell of her breasts.

He needed to get a grip here. Remember his priorities. One, he had to make sure she wasn't feeding a drug habit that might have driven her to snoop for classified information. Two, he had to deal with her insistence that she and Trixie Halston cohabited the same physical plane. Three—and most disturbing— there was that instant of pure malice in the restaurant. Drew didn't know what the hell to make of that.

It soon became apparent Tracy didn't, either. She looked exhausted and moved with a gingerly care that told him she was feeling the effects of her tumble down the cliffside this morning. Yet when he suggested she might want to take a long soak and make an early night of it, she threw a nervous glance at the bedroom and hedged.

"I'm not really tired. I'll just watch TV for a while, if that's all right."

"That's fine by me. Or we could listen to the rest of the radio broadcast."

"No!" Near panic flared in her eyes. She tried to cover it with a shaky laugh. "I've had enough of Trixie Halston tonight."

"Think the TV will keep her at bay?"

"I hope so!" She hesitated, looking embarrassed and uneasy at the same time. "To tell you the truth, she sort of creeped me out."

As if trying to subdue a sudden rash of goose bumps, Tracy massaged her upper arms. The brisk movement dragged back her sweater sleeves.

"Hell!"

Drew's curse froze her in midrub. Fright leaped into her eyes again.

"What is it? What's the matter?"

Gently, he pried her left arm loose and turned it over. The ugly red marks ringing her wrist made him feel like a Neanderthal on the loose.

"Christ, I'm sorry. I didn't intend to add to the bruises you collected when you fell this morning. Guess I got a little carried away at the restaurant."

His apology prompted a little gasp of relief from Tracy.

"So she weirded you out, too! Thank God! I thought... I was afraid..." She stopped, sucked in a sharp breath, and exhaled. "Okay, I admit it. I was afraid. Period."

Disgusted by the marks he'd left on her skin, Drew echoed the sentiment. "She had me sucking air for a while. Wait here. Charlie keeps some sports cream in the bathroom. He's not quite as spry at the helm of his boat as he used to be."

Drew was halfway across the room before the impact of his admission hit him. Damned if he wasn't starting to think of the woman at the restaurant as a separate entity.

Tracy watched him disappear into the bedroom and went limp with relief. He'd seen Trixie, too! More to the point, he'd absorbed her nasty vibes. Hugging his admission to her chest like a child would a torn, ragged blankie, she sank onto the L-shaped sofa.

She knew Drew hadn't wanted to believe her insistence that Trixie Halston had invaded her body. He'd as much as told her she'd gone off the rails. Tracy had pretty much decided the same thing. The knowledge that he'd seen *something* tonight lifted a huge weight from her shoulders.

She wasn't in this alone.

Kicking off her shoes, she curled her feet under her. Drew returned with a washcloth and a tube of sports cream.

"My wrist is fine. Really."

"It doesn't look fine. Scoot over."

She didn't remember experiencing any pain at the restaurant. Nor did she experience any now. Drew kept his touch incredibly gentle as he washed her bruises with the warm washcloth before applying the cream.

Tracy snaked her other arm along the back of the sofa. He was bent so close she could easily reach out and glide her fingers through his hair. The light from the lamp at the end of the sofa burnished it to a rich, dark mahogany that begged to be stroked.

It required considerable effort, but she resisted the impulse. She'd thrown herself at this man twice now. She wasn't completely sure how their first kiss had come about. She remembered something about offering him a taste of Juicy Fruit lipstick. Or maybe it was Passion Fruit.

But everything about the second kiss was etched in her mind with crystal clarity. She remembered moving with him to the smooth, mellow sounds of the orchestra. She recalled the play of his muscles under his shirt. Could still feel the sizzle that shot through her when her hip nudged the front of his jeans. Then he'd covered her mouth with his.

It hit her again—a jolt of pure hunger that made her squirm uncomfortably.

Drew's head came up. His eyebrows snapped together. "Am I hurting you?"

"No," she lied, banishing the memory of his mouth and tongue and hands. "I, uh, can feel the heat in the cream starting to work."

"It's good stuff. Charlie swears by it." He skimmed a glance over her face and shoulders. "Any other aches or pains you want me to work on?"

Little bubbles burst in her veins. She couldn't think of *anything* she wanted more right now than Drew's hands moving over her body. She opened her mouth to accept his offer, then clamped it shut.

She still didn't know what triggered Trixie Halston's sudden manifestations. What if the singer decided to pop out again? Tracy wasn't about to let Drew slather cream all over that woman. Ghost. Thing.

"Thanks for the offer, but I'll take a rain check. If I start to hurt, I'll let you know."

"You sure?" A grin slipped out, transforming the

rugged planes of his face. "I've been told I have pretty good hands."

Tracy struggled for breath. "I can vouch for that. My wrist feels better already."

Capping the tube, he tossed it on the coffee table and swiped his hands on the washcloth. She expected him to move to one of the easy chairs at that point, or at least to the other end of the sofa. Instead, he reached for the remote, kicked off his shoes and crossed his ankles on the sturdy table.

"Anything in particular you want to watch?"

She shook her head, too disconcerted by his proximity to care what came on the plasma screen. The images scrolled by in a blur of color and halted abruptly. The roar of fifty-thousand-plus fans filled the room.

Drew turned to her with a hopeful expression. "How do you feel about football?"

"Who's playing?"

"Notre Dame and Navy."

"The Irish stomped Navy last year." Uncurling her legs, she propped her feet next to his. "Fifty cents says they do it again."

"You're on."

Hiding her relief, Tracy settled into the soft suede. Her body craved sleep. The strain of taking care of Jack these past weeks had taken its toll. The situation she now found herself in was every bit as exhausting and far more frightening. As tired as she felt right now, though, she shied away from going into the bedroom.

She refused to admit she was afraid of who—or what—might be waiting for her. She *wasn't* ashamed to admit she hoped Drew's solid bulk would act as a shield to keep it at bay.

"Tracy."

The deep murmur drifted through layers of fog. Something warm stroked her hair.

"Wake up, sweetheart."

That penetrated. Opening her eyes to a bright wash of light, Tracy blinked owlishly and squinted at the blank TV screen.

"Who won?" she mumbled.

"Navy. You owe me fifty cents."

The hard pillow under her cheek shifted. She turned her head and Drew's face swam into focus above her.

"We need to get moving," he said, brushing the tangled hair away from her face. "We've got that appointment with Ed LaSorta at eleven."

"Eleven?"

Frowning, Tracy planted a hand on what she discovered was Drew's belly and pushed upright. Surprise dropped her jaw. That dazzling light didn't spill from the living room lamps. It poured through the crack in the drapes.

"What time is it?"

"Almost nine."

"You're kidding, right?"

"No, ma'am."

"Good Lord! I must have totally zoned out on you."

His mouth curved. "We both zoned out."

The realization she'd spent the night with her head cradled in Drew's lap warred for supremacy with Tracy's sudden awareness of how incredible he looked in the morning.

His shirt was wrinkled beyond belief. One tail hung over his belt. Stubble bristled on his cheeks and chin. His hair stood in short, dark spikes. If Tracy hadn't been so conscious of fuzz on her teeth and her own less than pristine appearance, she might have wiggled around in his lap and ravished him right then and there.

Reluctantly she relinquished her seat. "I'd better get cleaned up and changed."

Into what, she had no idea. She'd run out of clean clothes. Her trip to Catalina had extended well beyond the limits of her roll-on weekender.

With a jaw-cracking yawn, Drew stretched his arms over his head and loosened muscles that must have cramped from holding her all night. The tantalizing glimpse of the dark hair swirling around his belly button almost derailed Tracy's determination to brush her teeth before she took a bite out of him.

"I'll put on some coffee," he said, pushing off the sofa with lazy grace. "We can grab some breakfast en route to LaSorta's. Or wait and have lunch afterward. The LAPD detective we're going to meet with is in court until three. By the way, my friend Claire has cleared her schedule. She'll arrive tomorrow afternoon."

"When did you call her?"

"Last night, after you dropped off. So which is it? Breakfast or lunch?"

"Either one works for me." Tracy started for the bedroom, then paused. "Thanks, Drew."

"Hey, it was my pleasure. I never pass up the chance to spend a night with a beautiful woman draped across my lap."

"I appreciated the pillow service, but I wasn't referring to that."

"What, then?"

"For helping me on Catalina. For letting me stay here." She waved a hand in a vain attempt to encompass all the ways he'd come to her rescue. "For following through on the visits to LaSorta and the LAPD. For helping me prove Jack didn't kill that—" the word bitch popped into her head but she settled for "—that woman."

The smile went out of his eyes. "We're digging in to a sixty-year-old incident, Tracy. The chances of finding anything that points to a possible murder— much less a murderer—are slim at best."

"I know that. But thanks anyway."

"You're welcome. Now put it in gear, woman. I'm opting for breakfast."

Spurred by the stern admonition, Tracy started for

the bedroom once again. She made it only as far as the sofa table nestled against the wall, however. A sideways glance in the mirror above the fireplace stopped her cold. The apparition staring back at her sent her stomach plunging to the hardwood floor.

"Oh my *God!*"

Her dismayed shriek brought Drew running. His shirttail flapping, he rounded the counter between the kitchen and the living room at full speed. The expression on his face shook Tracy almost as much as the specter in the mirror. He looked like a man fully prepared to kill.

Both his speed and his expression altered when he spotted her. Eyes narrowed, he raked her with a quick, hard glance.

"What happened? Why did you scream?"

She aimed a shaking finger at the mirror. "I just got a look at myself."

"Oh, for…"

Shagging a hand through his hair, Drew waited for his heart to drop back into his chest. The incident in the restaurant last night had shaken him more than he'd let on. He'd spent half the night wondering how the hell to protect Tracy from herself, the other half counting all the reasons he shouldn't carry her into the bedroom and nudge her awake in ways that made him hot just to think about.

"No one looks like a supermodel after a night on a sofa," he said patiently. "But you come close, Tracy."

Damn close, in his considered opinion—if super-models came packaged in a neat, five-six frame and went for a rumpled, just-out-of-bed look.

"You don't understand." Her voice hitching, she gestured to the image in the mirror. "That's not me."

Drew's gut knotted. Oh, hell! Not again.

He'd searched Tracy's things again last night. More thoroughly, this time. He hadn't found so much as an aspirin among her clutter of cosmetics. That meant her hallucinations had to be homegrown.

"Look at her!" Planting her hands on her hips, she contemplated her image with withering scorn. "That puffed up hair. The mascara smears. The shadow caked in the creases of her eyes. She looks like a hooker." Her jaw tightened. "Correction, *I* look like a hooker."

She spun around, her eyes flashing green fire. "I gotta say, Trixie Halston is starting to get on my nerves."

"Yeah, well, she's doing a pretty good number on mine, too."

"Just tell me this. Which one of us fell asleep in your arms last night?"

That he could answer without doubt or hesitation. "You, Tracy."

"And who did you wake up with this morning?"

"You."

"That's all I needed to hear."

With a last, smoldering glance at the image in the mirror, she stomped into the bedroom.

Chapter 9

Edward LaSorta and Associates occupied two floors of a gleaming glass-and-steel tower in L.A.'s Century City. Fountains pulsed water fifty feet into the air at the entrance to the building. A glass-enclosed elevator shot Tracy and Drew skyward through a twenty-story atrium.

Publicity posters of the movies and television productions the LaSorta firm had done PR for lined the hallway leading to the executive suite of offices. Inside the suite, photos of the groups and individuals LaSorta had worked with formed an impressive rogues' gallery. The photos spanned the decades, from glamorous radio and television stars of the '40s and '50s to the grunge rock bands of today.

While Drew checked in with LaSorta's executive assistant, Tracy zeroed in on the photos from the '40s. She found a shot of Kenny Jones's orchestra, but it had been taken in 1943, several years after Trixie Halston's death. The photo showed the band members in flak vests and helmets, performing at some overseas base as part of a USO tour. Tracy didn't recognize the singer at the mike.

"If you'll follow me," the executive assistant said with a gracious smile, "I'll take you in to see Mr. LaSorta."

She led the way down a short hall paneled in marble and mahogany.

"Mr. LaSorta doesn't take many appointments anymore. We're so pleased he felt up to coming into the office today to take yours."

The comment made Tracy marvel again at Drew's pull. How many men in the classic car business maintained a standing entrée at a place like Nick's? Or got psychologists to make house calls? Or convinced an eightysomething semiretired PR exec to meet with him?

"Ms. Brandt and Mr. McDowell, sir."

"Come in, come in."

Edward LaSorta wheeled himself around his desk and greeted them with a handshake. "Please, have a seat."

"Would you like coffee?" his assistant asked as Tracy and Drew moved to sleek, black leather chairs grouped in front of tall windows with a bird's-eye view of downtown L.A. "Or tea perhaps?"

"I have a special brand of North Fujian oolong flown in from Hong Kong," LaSorta advised, maneuvering into position on the other side of a coffee table made from a rough-edged slab of black granite. "It's great for lowering blood pressure, improving digestion and promoting longevity."

The tea certainly seemed to be working for him. Tracy was amazed at how well the man wore his eighty-plus years. Constant exposure to the California sun—or expensive spas—had tanned his skin to tough, wrinkled leather. His blue eyes were cloudy, but he still boasted a full head of white hair. His charcoal-gray pinstriped suit shouted money. The Daffy Duck tie he wore with it suggested a lively sense of humor.

Both Tracy and Drew opted for the oolong. LaSorta's assistant withdrew to prepare the tea. Curiosity prompted their host to jump right into the reason for their visit.

"I understand you want to talk to me about one of the bands I worked with."

"That's right," Drew confirmed. "The Kenny Jones Orchestra."

"Kenny Jones?" Surprise stretched LaSorta's leathery skin. "What's your interest in him?"

"Actually, we're more interested in one of his lead singers. Trixie Halston."

"Who?"

Tracy's heart sank at his blank expression. Fighting a sharp sense of disappointment, she leaned forward and supplied the pertinent details.

"Trixie Halston sang with the Kenny Jones Orchestra from 1939 to 1941. She also recorded a single of the hit song 'I'll Walk Alone.'"

"Sorry, I don't remember a girl singer by that… Oh, wait a minute!" He smacked his forehead. "Wasn't she the canary who took a dive from the balcony of the Avalon Ballroom?"

"Yes."

"God! Trixie Halston. Must be forty, fifty years since I heard that name."

Much as she was coming to dislike the singer, Tracy felt a sneaking twinge of sorrow on her behalf. How had Jack put it? Her star had never had a chance to really shine.

"That woman was a piece of work," LaSorta mused, dredging up distant memories.

"How so?"

"She was what we'd term high-strung today. On top of the world one minute, in the dumps the next." He winked one cloudy blue eye. "Liked to drive the occasional Cadillac, if you know what I mean."

"No," Tracy admitted, "I don't."

"A Cadillac is what we used to call an ounce packet of heroin."

"Trixie used heroin?"

"Most all of the musicians did. Heroin or cocaine. Still do, for that matter. Trixie wasn't any exception. Kenny wasn't sure half the time whether she would show for a gig. And then there were the men." He shook his head. "She reeled 'em in like fish. Especially the sailors."

"Do you by any chance remember one particular sailor by the name of Jack Foster? He was in the merchant marines."

Forehead furrowed, LaSorta searched his memory bank and came up empty. "No, sorry."

"She might have called him John. Or Johnny."

"Doesn't ring a bell. Like I said, the boys in uniform were always sniffing around her skirts."

"She was in love with this one. They talked about getting married."

"If you say so."

At that point, his assistant returned carrying an enameled tray. With calm efficiency, she tipped a delicate porcelain teapot and poured steaming, champagne-colored liquid into three handless cups.

"Would you care for lemon or milk?" she asked Tracy.

"Neither, thank you."

Beaming his approval at her correct answer, LaSorta waited until they'd all been served and his assistant had departed once again to pick up the thread of their conversation.

"Why are you so interested in Trixie's love life?"

"Jack Foster was sort of an uncle to me," Tracy replied. "He died recently. At his request, I took his ashes to Catalina and scattered them on a hillside. That's when I learned about Trixie Halston and how *she* died."

"Real tragic, that accident. A real waste, too. The kid might have made something of herself. She could sure warble out a tune."

"That's what it was?" Drew asked, easing into the conversation. "An accident?"

"She leaned over too far, lost her balance and fell. That's the spin I put on it, anyway. Would have looked bad for the band if it leaked that their singer was so hopped up she thought she could fly."

"Did the police do a tox screen of her blood?"

"I'm not sure they had that kind of technology back then. But the cornet player admitted sharing a Cadillac with her before they went on that night. What the heck was his name? Gabe? Gary?"

"Gus," Drew supplied. "Gus Rosendorf."

"That's him! Good man on the horn, as I recall. More tea, Ms. Brandt?"

"No, thanks." Tracy locked her hands around her cup. "Mr. LaSorta, did the police uncover any evidence to indicate someone night have pushed Trixie Halston over the balcony?"

"Not a shred." He peered at her through the steam rising from his refreshened tea. "Why? Did this friend of yours… What was his name?"

"Jack Foster."

"Did Jack tell you otherwise?"

"He never mentioned Trixie Halston at all until right before he died. At that point, his memory was hazy at best."

"So what's with all these questions? Excuse my bluntness, but what difference does it make after so many years *how* Halston died?"

She could hardly blurt out that Trixie had come back from the dead to accuse her former lover. Or that she was making her life hell in the process. Squirming a little, Tracy tiptoed around the question.

"It's become something of a personal quest. In my uncle's memory, I'm going to keep digging until I'm certain I have the truth."

"You are, huh? Well, I wish you good luck." Setting down his cup, he shifted uncomfortably. "Damned wheelchair. You'd think they'd pad the seats or something. Sorry, folks. Anything else I can do for you?"

"I guess not." Tracy returned her cup to the tray and rose. "Thank you so much for your time."

Drew did the same. "If you remember anything else about Ms. Halston's death, please give us a call. We'll be in town for a few days."

"Where are you staying?"

"The Marina Del Ray Towers, unit twelve-fifteen.

You can call us there or on my cell phone. Your assistant has both numbers."

"If I think of anything, I'll get in touch."

After a late lunch, they made a stop at the homicide division of the Los Angeles Police Department. Since Trixie Halston's death had been ruled an accident, the LAPD had closed her case file and buried it in the archives.

"Took some digging to find it," Detective Dan Riley told them. A big man with a splotchy purple birthmark over his right eyebrow, he tipped a dog-eared manila folder and slid the contents onto his desk. "I've got the responding officer's report, the investigative team's findings and the coroner's determination as to cause of death. Pretty obvious, when you see the pictures. They're not pretty," he warned with a glance in Tracy's direction.

Despite the caution, the image of the singer's broken body sprawled obscenely on the rocks made her stomach heave. Bile rose in bitter waves. She swallowed convulsively, fighting to keep it down, fighting the almost overpowering urge to weep and wail and shriek as well.

OhGodohGodohGod!

Pain splintered through her. Rage piled on top of despair, putting unbearable pressure on her chest. She couldn't breathe, couldn't look away from the blood-soaked gown and hair spilling out of a golden snood. Like a snarling beast, something ripped and clawed at her insides.

Trixie. It was Trixie, battling to get out, vicious in her fury.

No! No, dammit!

She wouldn't give in this time. Wouldn't let the beast devour her. Wrapping her arms around her middle, Tracy fought with every ounce of will she possessed.

Still it raged, almost suffocating her with its violence. She felt her hold on herself slipping. The photo blurred. The room spun. Inch by terrifying inch, she slid toward the dark abyss.

"Tracy?"

The sound of her name pierced the fury. She grabbed at it like a lifeline, clinging with the desperation of a drowning man about to be swallowed by a dark, raging sea.

Did you hear that, you witch? Drew called to me. Me!

"Tracy, sweetheart." A warm hand reached for hers. A strong, sure grip anchored her. "Are you okay?"

With a low, keening wail, the fury subsided. The room stopped spinning. Her eyes refocused. Digging deep inside, she found the strength to squeeze Drew's hand.

"Sorry."

Her smile was wobbly, but it was hers. All hers.

"I, uh, had a little sinking spell."

"I'm not surprised." Riley shuffled the crime-scene photos under the stack of reports. "All the cases I've worked, the blood and gore still get to me, too."

"What's this?" Drew asked, easing an opaque paper bag from under the stack. Inside was another slip of paper covered with rust-colored stains.

"That's a handwritten note. According to the evidence log, it was found in the pocket of Halston's dress."

"Mind if I take a look?"

"Be my guest. I've got some latex gloves in my bottom drawer."

Drew snapped on the gloves and slid the note out of the paper bag. Tracy's nostrils twitched at the faint, iron scent that came with it. When she identified the odor as dried blood, her belly rolled again. Fists clenched, she battled the stirring beast into submission while Drew carefully unfolded the note.

"Sonofabitch."

His fierce mutter produced startled glances from both Tracy and the detective. They leaned in and peered at the faint, almost indiscernible handwriting.

"The *Kallister*," Riley read aloud. "What's a *Kallister?*"

"It's a U.S. cargo ship," Drew replied, his jaw tight. "Manned and operated by the merchant marines. She was torpedoed off the coast of California on November nineteenth, 1941."

"The day after the Halston woman died," Riley commented. "What's the connection?"

"I don't know."

But he sure as hell intended to find out. His mind whirling, Drew held the gory note up to the light.

"Did the crime-scene folks check this for prints?"

"They did. They found Halston's prints all over it and another set they couldn't identify."

Drew wasn't sure what access investigators had to fingerprint files sixty-five years ago, but the databases had expanded exponentially since then.

"Do me a favor, would you, and run the prints through the automated fingerprint identification system. I'd also like you to spray the note with Ninhydrin. If you lift any oil residue, run the DNA, too."

"Can do. Might take a day or two, though. Where can I reach you?"

"We're at the Marina Del Ray."

Extracting a business card, Drew scribbled the condo's phone number on the back. Riley flipped the card over and angled back in his chair.

"Classic Motors, Incorporated, huh?" He fingered the embossed lettering, his eyes speculative under the purple birthmark. "Mind telling me how a man who makes his living restoring old cars knows about AFIS and Ninhydrin?"

Tracy was asking herself the same question.

"I read a lot of cop thrillers."

"Do you?" Riley tapped the card against his palm. "That doesn't explain why my boss got a call that put a bug up his ass—'scuse the French, Ms. Brandt—

and mine. He didn't say who the call was from, only that I was to give you every possible assistance."

"Which I appreciate," Drew said, rising. "Any time I can return the favor, just call that number."

Curling a hand under Tracy's elbow, he escorted her through the homicide division's endless rows of gray cubicles. Once in the tiled hallway, he tugged her around.

"You sure you're okay? You looked like you were about to keel over there for a minute."

"It was Trixie. She wanted out. I wouldn't let her use me this time."

His expression went from frowning concern to careful neutrality. "Trixie, huh?"

"You still don't believe me? After what happened at the restaurant last night? You felt her presence, Drew. I *know* you did."

"All right, I felt something. I'm just not ready to admit it was a ghost."

Hurt and more than a little pissed by his skepticism after all they'd been through, she angled her chin. "What was it, then?"

"I'm damned if I know. I'm hoping Claire can tell us."

"Who?"

"Claire Cantwell. Dr. Claire Cantwell," he amended. "The psychologist I told you about."

Grasping her elbow again, he steered her toward the entrance. Tracy waited until they'd left the snarl of downtown L.A. and cruised onto Marina Parkway to voice a few doubts of her own.

"You didn't answer Detective Riley's question about the phone call."

"He didn't ask one, just probed politely for information."

"I won't be so polite. Who made the call to his boss and got LAPD to open its doors to us?"

"A friend."

"Another friend? You've certainly got a wide circle of acquaintances. Powerful acquaintances, from the sound of it."

"Some are," he said with a shrug. "Some are just ordinary folks, like me."

"Ordinary folks don't own vacation condos in one of L.A.'s priciest neighborhoods."

"It's not a vacation condo. It's a place Charlie and I use when we have business in L.A."

Annoyed by his deliberate vagueness, Tracy pressed harder.

"Who are you, Drew? Why does everyone jump when you say the word? And why the heck are you putting your life on hold to help me?"

"I'll take the last one first. I thought my reasons for putting my life on hold became painfully obvious last night. I've got a serious case of the hots for you, Brandt."

It took Tracy a few moments to recover. By that time the tall palms of the marina were swaying into view.

"Okay, I can buy that. The feeling's mutual, by the way. What about the rest of it? Who are you, Andrew McDowell?"

"How about I answer your questions after you answer Claire's?"

"Dammit, Drew—"

"After you talk to Claire," he said firmly.

Dr. Cantwell wasn't the only one who showed up at the condo the following afternoon. She'd brought an associate. The breezy, dark-haired woman dumped several larges cases in the foyer, waved hello to a surprised Drew and offered Tracy her hand.

"Mackenzie Blair. Hope you don't mind that I butted in on this case."

"Well, I…"

"I'm a communications specialist. When Claire mentioned she was coming to the coast to talk to someone who might be receiving communications from, uh, the psychic world, I had to come along to see if I could record them."

The psychologist also came forward to shake hands. A slender woman with silvery blond hair and a serene air, she offered a counterpoint to the brunette's vivacious energy.

"You don't have to decide the issue of recording our conversations right this moment, Ms. Brandt. We'll talk, get to know each other a little, and proceed only if you feel comfortable."

Tracy looked to Drew.

"It's your call," he told her. "But I can vouch for Mac. She's a—"

"Don't tell me. I can guess. She's a friend."

"One of the best," he replied with a grin.

Chapter 10

Claire banished Drew and Mackenzie to the marina so she and Tracy could talk. Instructing them to return in two hours, she shrugged off the jacket of her amethyst silk pants suit and stepped out of her pumps.

"Let's get comfortable."

Claiming one end of the suede sectional, she tucked her legs under her. Tracy chose the easy chair and put the coffee table between them. The psychologist's calm air and friendly smile invited confidence, but the very distinct possibility the blonde might decide Tracy was psychotic and required restraint hovered over her like the blade of a guillotine.

She'd keep her distance, physically *and* emotionally, until she knew she could trust this woman.

Cantwell didn't seem perturbed by her deliberate separation. "What has Drew told you about me?"

"Only that you're a friend. He seems to have a lot of them."

"Yes, he does. He's a good man. Would you like to know my professional credentials?"

"I guess that's as good a place as any to start."

"I have a bachelor's and master's in clinical psychology from Penn State and a Ph.D. in cognitive neuroscience from Yale. I practiced clinical psychology until my first husband was taken for ransom and killed during a bungled rescue attempt in Venezuela. Since then I've become something of an expert in the field of crisis negotiations."

Tracy's gaze dropped to the sparkling solitaire on her ring finger. With the light bouncing off its square-cut surface, the rock was hard to miss.

"I've recently remarried," she explained with a smile. "Luis—my husband—is also a good friend of Drew's."

"I'm starting to feel surrounded."

Her light, musical laugh filled the living room. "I can understand why. Is there anything else you'd like to know about me?"

"Just one thing, Dr. Cantwell."

"Please, call me Claire. May I call you Tracy?"

She waited for a nod before continuing. "What would you like to know?"

Deciding she might as well get it right out in the open, Tracy voiced her worry. "What happens if you decide I'm seriously delusional? Am I going to leave here in a straitjacket?"

"There is that possibility, of course."

The blunt response had the contradictory effect of settling Tracy's nerves. She gave the woman high marks for refusing to lie to her.

Claire turned the question back to her. "Do you think you're seriously delusional?"

"No. Well, maybe. A little. What has Drew told you about *me?*"

"I know you've recently lost someone very close to you," she said gently. "I also know you got fired from your job because you took off to care for him. That kind of physical and emotional stress can manifest itself in a variety of ways."

Tracy snatched desperately at that straw. "You think that's my problem? I'm stressed out?"

"It's far too soon for me to form an opinion. Why don't you just tell me what's going on?"

"It's this big band singer who died in 1941. Trixie Halston. She pops into my head—and my body—and sort of takes over."

"How long has she been entering your consciousness?"

"Four… No, five days now."

God, it seemed so much longer! Tracy almost couldn't remember life before Trixie Halston.

"So this is a recent occurrence?"

"Very. I never heard of the woman until I visited the Avalon Ballroom on Catalina Island. That's where she died. I think that's also where my uncle met her, right before the outbreak of World War II."

"Do you know when she's with you?"

"I didn't at first. Then I began to feel her rage and pain."

"Why is she angry?"

"She believes she was murdered." Gulping, Tracy forced out the rest. "By my Uncle Jack."

"She told you he killed her?"

"Yes. Or rather she told Drew. Two nights ago at the restaurant. I could feel her fury, hear myself mouthing her words."

Kicking off her shoes, Tracy hooked her heels on the edge of her chair and wrapped her arms around her knees. She knew darn well a protective crouch wouldn't keep the beast at bay, but she went into one anyway.

"I felt her again yesterday, when Drew and I were at LAPD headquarters. The detective showed me police photos taken after she fell."

Shudders ripped through her. Hugging her knees, Tracy propped her chin on them and held on.

"She wanted out then in the worst way. I felt as though she was clawing at my insides, trying to tear through my skin."

The psychologist's delicately penciled eyebrows rose. "But you kept her in?"

"I kept her in."

"I see."

"I'm glad you do, because I sure as heck don't! Where is she coming from, Dr. Cantwell? Claire?"

"Again, it's far too soon for me to form an opinion. All I can say at this point is that the human brain is a marvelously complex system. It contains over ten billion neuron cells, all connected in countless loops that feed and process information. More than a hundred different chemicals stimulate the transmission of that information. Scientists haven't begun to understand how these transmitters and neurons interact. We do know, however, that electromagnetic misfiring in the temporal lobe can cause a person to feel an expanded sense of their universe. Many have described it as a paranormal experience much like yours."

"Electromagnetic misfiring? Is that a polite way of saying I've short-circuited?"

"Something like that," she said with a smile. "Given your recent emotional trauma, you might have created a mental juxtaposition between your uncle's death and Trixie Halston's. But there are gaps you can't fill in, which may in turn be adding to your trauma."

"Can you run some sort of test? See if we can find the gaps?"

"Actually, I'd like to conduct several tests. The first is the MMPI-2—the Minnesota Multiphasic Personality Inventory, second revision. I'd also like to observe your sleep cycles to see how often you enter a hypnagogic state."

"And that is…?"

"The short interval between deep sleep and waking up, when we're not quite fully conscious. We often continue to dream, yet think we're awake."

"Been there, done that," Tracy admitted.

"We all have. We might also try some deep relaxation techniques. Perhaps hypnosis. How does all that sound to you?"

"Very time-consuming. How long are you planning to remain in L.A.?"

"As long as you want me to."

Tracy dropped her feet to the fluffy area rug. "Look, Claire, your friendship with Drew is one thing. Imposing on a mental health professional with your credentials is something else again. We'd better discuss your fee before we proceed any further."

The slender blonde didn't insult Tracy by brushing aside her concern.

"I'm working on a paper for the *American Journal of Psychology* that deals with cognitive disassociation of the sort we're discussing here. With your permission, I'd like to include our sessions as part of my research. I promise you complete anonymity, of course."

"That's it? That's all you want from me? Permission to include me in your study?"

"Not everyone cares to see their deepest fears and

anxieties in print," Claire said quietly. "I'm actually asking a great deal. Perhaps you'd like to think about it for a while? Or talk to Drew?"

"Drew's the reason we're both sitting here. I'm in if you are, Doc."

"Good! I'll fetch my briefcase and we'll get started."

Drew stretched an arm along the back of the blue-cushioned seat, his hand wrapped around an icy beer. The deck of Charlie's twin-diesel, twenty-six-foot *Kingfisher* rocked gently beneath his soles.

That business about the bloodstained note found in Trixie Halston's pocket bugged the hell out of him. Why the *Kallister?* Did the singer have some interest in the ship besides the fact her lover and alleged killer was assigned to it?

Hopefully, Detective Riley would lift some hard evidence from that note. In the meantime, Drew had asked Denise to contact MARAD—the U.S. Department of Transportation's Maritime Administration. He wanted a list of all ships that had sailed from the same port as the *Kallister* six months before and after Halston's death. He wasn't sure what he'd do with the information when he got it, but his gut told him there was more to that note than mere coincidence.

In the meantime, all he could do was wait and share a beer with his boss's wife. Mackenzie sat slouched in a captain's swivel chair a few feet away.

Looking as sleek and feline as a panther with her dark hair and tall, supple frame clothed all in black, she had her eyes closed and her face tipped to the bright California sun.

"Lord, this feels good. It had started to sleet just before we left D.C."

"I'm surprised your plane got out."

"It was touch-and-go for a while."

"I'm also surprised Lightning sent you out here with Cyrene."

"He didn't send me. I convinced him this was the perfect opportunity for me to test a new thermal emission spectrometer recently developed by NASA."

"You're going to test it on Tracy?"

"That's the plan."

"Is this thing safe?"

"All it does is measure heat emissions." She opened one eye. "Why? Am I hearing more than a professional concern for the target here, Riev?"

"She's had a rough time in the past few weeks. Even rougher the past few days. I don't want her hurt."

Mackenzie glommed on to his brusque response like a Doberman on to a shinbone. Both eyes open now, she wiggled upright.

"Omigosh! Can it be? Has the mighty Riever finally fallen? The stalwart oak who resisted the charms of every woman I've hooked him up with over the years? The lone wolf who thinks one divorce is enough for a lifetime?"

"Gimme a break, Mac. I just met Tracy a few days ago."

"So?"

"So we haven't made it to the marriage *or* divorce stage yet."

Hell, they hadn't even made it into bed. Drew had spent one night alone in his hotel room fantasizing about the woman, the next with her head nestled in his lap. He'd counted every dark lash, every freckle, every restless twitch that telegraphed an instant, urgent signal from his groin to his brain. Drew got off the sofa yesterday morning wanting her with a craving that went beyond physical.

They'd kept their distance last night, each in separate rooms. The separation hadn't stopped him from thinking about her, though. The woman's raw courage only added to her appeal. Drew had witnessed her fierce battle with herself, had seen how she handled what had to be a terrifying situation. There was something inside her, something angry and violent, fighting to get out.

He couldn't put a label on what that something was. Hopefully, Claire could. Maybe she'd diagnose a case of multiple personalities. Or extreme transference. Or a grief so deep Tracy had spun an elaborate fantasy to maintain a tie, however bizarre, to her friend, Jack. Whatever was inside her, it was ripping her apart.

Drew just wasn't ready to buy into the idea of a ghost. He knew there were huge gaps in man's understanding of his universe, but he'd grown up working with his hands, first in his father's garage, then as a machinist's mate in the navy, now in the business he shared with Charlie. Along the way, he'd collected bachelor's and master's degrees in engineering. He understood the laws of physics. Believed there was a rational explanation for 99.9 percent of seemingly irrational or random acts.

His years as an OMEGA operative had reinforced that belief. Sure, sheer dumb luck came into play at times. Without the skill and instincts to capitalize on that luck, however, an agent would be up the creek.

Sort of like Drew was now. He'd all but resolved his doubts about Tracy's interest in the *Kallister* back there on Catalina. This business with Trixie Halston and the note found in her pocket had opened them up again.

"Tracy's my target," he reminded OMEGA's chief techie. "You know as well as I do it's not smart to get involved with someone you've been sent to scope out."

"She doesn't have any idea you're lusting for her?"

"She's not stupid, Mac. She knows I'm attracted to her."

No need to confess he'd come right out and *told* Tracy he had the hots for her. Mackenzie would jump on that with unholy glee.

"Does she know you've taken her under your wing for reasons other than the kindness of your heart?"

"Is that a slur on my skill as an undercover operative?"

"More like a caution. I don't know the target, but as you said, she's no dummy. How's she going to react if she finds out you've had her under a microscope the whole time you've been together?"

Drew had started asking himself the same thing around dawn yesterday morning. About the time he realized having Tracy zoned out on his lap, her hair spilling across his thighs, satisfied a need to protect her almost as deep and fierce as the urge to carry her into the bedroom.

"I'll just have to make sure she doesn't find out."

Mackenzie bit back a flippant reply. She'd worked with Riever for going on six years now. He rarely talked about his brief marriage and shrugged off the notion that he was still carrying the scars.

Yet Mac couldn't count the number of female friends she'd paraded in front of him, hoping one would hold his interest for longer than a few weeks or a month. She'd even tried to enlist her husband in her determined campaign. Nick, bless his diplomatic soul, had told her to back off and butt out.

The possibility that Riever might have fallen for Tracy Brandt raised all kinds of possibilities in Mac's fertile mind. And all kinds of problems. Not the least was Brandt's reaction if she discovered Riev had been hanging with her for reasons other than simple animal attraction. Eager to get to know the woman who'd brought him to his knees, Mac yanked back the cuff of her black turtleneck.

"Cyrene said to come back in two hours. It's past that. I say we head upstairs."

Drew confirmed the designated interval had passed, tipped up his beer and drained it. "I'll get the *Kingfisher* squared away and battened down."

Mac lent an able hand. Like Drew, she'd spent some time in uniform but often joked that they'd served in different navies. Her experience as a communications officer was a world apart from his as a machinist's mate.

"We've completed phase one," Claire announced when Drew and Mac reentered the condo.

Her eyes intent behind the lenses of her half glasses, she sat at the kitchen table in front of a small, sleek laptop. What looked like a multipage, multiple-choice exam sat beside the laptop.

"Where's Tracy?"

"In the other room, taking a much-needed bathroom break."

Drew dragged out a chair for Mac and one for himself. Straddling his, he propped his elbows on the back and lowered his voice.

"What's your take so far?"

Claire slid her glasses down to the tip of her nose. Since joining OMEGA, she'd learned to walk the fine line between her obligations as a practicing psychologist and her responsibilities as an agent.

She'd promised Tracy complete confidentiality.

She'd hold to that promise. She'd also made it clear she was here at Drew's request. When asked, Tracy hadn't voiced any objection to Claire's sharing general impressions with him or Mac.

"My take is that we're dealing with a very intelligent woman who's endured tremendous stress in recent months. I won't know for sure until I interpret her MMPI, but my initial impression is that she doesn't *appear* to suffer from any cognitive or personality disorder."

"What about this business with the ghost?"

"As I said, I need to interpret the MMPI."

"How long will that take?"

"Several hours. I was going to suggest you take Tracy and Mac out for a long, leisurely dinner while I do."

"What about you? You need to eat, too."

"I'll order in a pizza or something. When you return, I want to try some relaxation techniques. Perhaps hypnosis. Mac, Tracy has agreed to let you document those sessions."

Mac's eyes lit up. "Great! I brought a bagful of new toys I want to test. I'll split that pizza with you, Cyrene. I need to set up my equipment and make sure it's fully charged and ready to record."

That left just Drew and Tracy.

The anticipation that licked at his veins should have prompted Drew to suggest they *all* stay in and chow down on pizza. Tracy's pale face and tired smile when she emerged from the bathroom deep-sixed that notion.

She looked as if Claire had put her through a mental wringer. Judging by the number of pages in that multiple-choice questionnaire stacked beside her laptop, she probably had. And there were more tests yet to come.

Drew hated that he'd been the one to insist Tracy go through all this. The urge to protect her, to soothe away those tired lines, clashed more and more with his need to pinpoint her precise interest in the *Kallister*. His protective instincts won out this time.

"Claire says I should take you out for a long, relaxing meal. She needs to tote up your score on the tests she administered."

Her smile wavered. "I'm not up for Nick's. Not after the last time."

"I was thinking more along the lines of take-out Chinese and a sunset cruise up the coast. Mac and I idled away the last couple of hours aboard my ex-father-in-law's boat. All the *Kingfisher* needs is gas and she's ready to go."

"That sounds wonderful."

"Get your windbreaker. It'll turn cool once the sun goes down."

Chapter 11

As it turned out, the *Kingfisher* never left its slip.

By the time Drew placed a to-go order at Ding How, one of many restaurants on the boulevard facing the marina, and made a stop at a minimart to pick up some rubber-soled boat shoes for Tracy, the sun had already begun to sink toward the horizon. Drew was all for taking the *Kingfisher* out anyway, but the string of in-coming watercraft lined up at the floating service platform torpedoed his plans.

"Sorry. I should have guessed from the banners announcing the three-day fishing derby that we'd have a traffic jam about this time."

"That's okay. It feels good just to be out in the open air."

"Want to eat on deck or in the cabin?"

"On deck, if it's not too much trouble."

"No trouble at all." He deposited the bag containing their supper on a deck locker. "Let me switch on the power, then I'll set up the table."

"What can I do?"

"Just enjoy the view."

That was easy enough. While Drew puttered below deck, Tracy spun in a slow circle to absorb the spectacle of hundreds of fishing and sailing boats nestled in their slips. Their forest of masts and antennas formed an almost impenetrable barrier between shore and sea.

The *Kingfisher* was moored in the last slip on the dock, some hundred or so yards from a massive stone breakwater that guarded the entrance to the marina. Beyond the low wall, the Pacific rolled in endless waves.

The view from the condo's twelfth floor had stolen Tracy's breath. But being here on the water, at the edge of the open sea, made her feel almost as if she were a part of that restless, rolling tide.

She leaned her elbows on the grab rail and made a determined attempt to slough off her weariness. What would it be like to just drift on that tide? Go wherever it took her? Not worry about finding a job or paying next month's rent or exorcising a ghost?

Not cringe inside every time she said Trixie's name and Drew assumed that careful, neutral expression? Nothing like spending the night with your head in the lap of a man who thought you'd blown at least one fuse.

Smart, girl. Real smart.

What made it worse was that she ached to repeat the experience. She couldn't remember the last time she'd felt so... So safe.

"You look like you'd like to crank the engine, cast off the lines and set the compass for due west."

Angling her head, she found Drew paused halfway up the steps from the cabin. One elbow rested on the side of the hatch. The breeze ruffled his dark hair. His face was cast in shades of bronze by the sun.

Okay, so he didn't just make her feel safe. He made her feel hungry. And not for Chinese take-out.

With some effort, she disguised the sudden surge of heat in her belly behind a smile. "You pegged it. I was just imagining what it would be like to drift on the tide for a few weeks or months or years."

"A few weeks at sea aren't bad. A few months are tolerable. A year or more is another story. Just ask any sailor. The navy has the highest divorce rate of all the military services."

Belatedly she remembered Drew mentioning that his tours of sea duty had upset his ex-wife.

"Is that what caused your divorce? The long separations?"

"They didn't help. Joyce and I got married after a short, crazy courtship and lived together all of three months before I shipped out the first time. We grew older—if not wiser—with several oceans between us."

Emerging from the hatch, he inserted a short pole into a socket in the aft section of the deck, then went back down for a lightweight tabletop. Tracy helped him position and anchor the table. While she set out the cartons of jade shrimp and Szechwan beef they'd carried aboard, he went below again.

She heard a static-filled buzz as Drew surfed several radio stations before settling on one that played classic rock. Her hips swaying to the rhythm of the Moody Blues, she emptied the carryout bag of a large foam container of hot tea, packets of soy, duck and mustard sauce and cellophane-wrapped chopsticks.

He emerged again with paper plates and plastic forks. "Guess we won't need these," he said, eyeing the chopsticks.

"You might not, but I will. I've never mastered the art of wielding those sticks."

"All it requires is a simple lever action." Easing onto the cushioned bench, he punched a set from their wrapper. "Have a seat and I'll demonstrate."

Tracy slid in beside him. All too aware of his thigh brushing hers, she tried to concentrate on the impromptu lesson.

"Wedge one stick in the *V* of your hand and anchor it between your second and third fingers. Hold it still with the lower portion of your thumb."

"Like this?"

"That's it. Now take the other one. You want to work it with the upper part of your thumb and first finger."

He clicked his chopsticks together at few times. Tracy's missed each other completely.

"Keep the bottom one tight. Here, I'll show you."

Laying aside his wooden implements, he covered her hand with his. Warmth flowed from the surface of his skin to hers, and Tracy lost her limited ability to manipulate the sticks.

"It's no use. I'm all thumbs."

Drew wouldn't allow her to admit defeat. "You'll get the hang of it."

"I'll probably starve to death in the process."

"We can't let that happen."

Dumping a portion of the jade shrimp onto a plate, he corrected her fumbling attempts to spear a morsel.

"Don't stab, squeeze. Now take a bite."

His hand guiding hers, he delivered the succulent shrimp to within a few inches of Tracy's mouth. She leaned in, her shoulder to his chest, and nibbled at the tender morsel.

"Good?"

"Mmm."

Downing the shrimp, she chased a snow pea around her plate. It defeated her best attempts, forcing Drew to take a hand again. He was grinning when he fed her the crunchy green pod.

But when she took it between her lips, the cocky glint left his eyes. They stayed locked on her mouth for so long Tracy had trouble swallowing.

"I, uh, think I've figured out the lever action you were talking about."

"Show me."

Stretching his arm along the back of the seat cushion, he gave her room to maneuver. It took several attempts before she flourished a shrimp between the two wooden spears.

"Ta-daaa!"

Flush with victory, she offered him the pink-and-white tidbit. Drew's strong white teeth crunched down. The shrimp disappeared. He chewed for a moment, then washed it down with a swig of tea.

Tracy followed the movement of his Adam's apple and felt her own throat close. When she lifted her gaze to his, she saw a hunger that matched hers in the skin stretched taut across his cheekbones.

Tracy knew she shouldn't lean in again. Shouldn't glide her tongue along his lower lip. So much had happened in the short time they'd known each other. So much she couldn't explain. So much that scared the crap out of her.

But Drew was the one constant in all that turmoil. The voice of calm reason. The heat that melted her icy fear. Whatever Claire's tests revealed, whatever tomorrow brought, he was here with her now. For this moment.

Surrendering to the fierce need to lose herself in him for however long she could, she dropped her chopsticks, leaned in and feasted on his mouth. He answered with a skill that sent tight, hot spasms spearing into her belly.

One kiss wasn't enough. It wasn't anywhere *near* enough. They were almost horizontal on the cushions when Tracy gasped for breath.

"Maybe... Maybe we should move our picnic to the cabin."

His eyes darkened. The skin stretched tighter across his cheeks. She could see him wrestling with his own doubts, hear the warning in his low growl.

"If we go below deck, it won't be to play with chopsticks."

"I know."

The soft whisper acted like a trigger. He was on his feet in one fluid move. Tugging Tracy up, he crushed her mouth with his.

They were tearing at each other's clothes before they reached the hatch. He left his red windbreaker on the short flight of steps leading down to the cabin. Tracy's pea-green jacket hit the galley floor. Her sweater followed an instant later.

She formed a dim impression of polished teak and gleaming brass. A bank of radios and blank screens passed in a blur. The tang of varnish and mildew and bilge water tickled her nostrils. Her hip collided with the rounded corner of a built-in.

With the radio pulsing to the beat of The Beatles' "Yellow Submarine," Drew pressed her into the cushions of a narrow sofa. In a fever of need, Tracy popped the snap of his jeans and attacked his zipper. He stripped off her canvas deck shoes and slacks with equal ferocity.

When he got up to shuck the last of his clothing, she levered herself onto one elbow. The combination of rippling muscle, swirling chest hair and rock-hard erection stopped the breath in her throat. It left on a gasp when she spotted the scar slashing across three of his ribs.

"Drew! What happened to you?"

"Very old, very embarrassing story." Reaching around her, he unhooked her bra with smooth dexterity. "Take it from me, you should never get on the bad side of a DeWALT three-eighty sheet metal jigsaw."

The wound didn't look all that old to Tracy, but the feel of his hands and mouth on her breasts soon drove the ugly scar out of her head.

Determined to keep it out, Drew hooked an arm around her waist and stretched her out on the cushions. He hadn't lied to her. He did get careless with a jigsaw years ago. The glancing cut had left a small scar. That old, long-healed scar had disappeared into another last year, compliments of the machete-wielding bastard who'd lunged out of a darkened doorway in a Manila alley.

This wasn't the time to go into details, though. Not with Tracy sleek and supple beneath him and the twin mounds of her breasts his to plunder. Stretching out alongside her, he did just that.

Her nipples unfolded into stiff points. The ache in Drew's groin intensified with every flick of his tongue, but he kept his touch light and tormenting. Tracy's breath was coming hard and fast when he palmed the smooth skin of her belly.

Contorting, he nipped at the warm flesh. Her back arched. Her belly hollowed under his hand. Her body's instinctive, uninhibited response elicited a low growl from Drew.

"You make me want to do things to you that are still illegal in six states."

Her laugh was husky and ragged around the edges. "I won't tell if you don't."

If Drew had needed any additional incentive, he got it when he peeled down her panties and spotted the wafer-thin patch on her lower abdomen. Small and square and just a little gummy around the edges, it shouted that she was prepared for any and all eventualities.

Kneeing her legs apart, he fingered her slick flesh. She was wet and eager, but small. And tight. Very tight. Using his fingers and thumb, Drew primed her.

"Oh!"

Her head went back. A groan ripped from deep in her throat. The small convulsions that shook her provoked an instant response from Drew. Positioning himself between her thighs, he thrust home.

A loud rumble from the vicinity of Drew's middle pierced his lazy contentment. It also prompted a giggle from the woman sprawled half-under and half-beside him.

"Now it's your turn. My stomach was the one making noises that day on Catalina."

Her laughter was so normal, so girlish, that his heart turned over inside his chest.

She'd been through so much in the past few weeks. After losing both her job and the man she'd loved and cared for, she was now caught in a cruel mental vise. Drew ached to keep her here, sheltered aboard the *Kingfisher*, but duty in the form of Cyrene and Mac called.

Dipping his head, he nuzzled the niche between her neck and shoulder. "Guess we ought to go topside before the gulls devour our supper."

"Guess so."

She didn't stir except to trail a fingertip along his backbone. He wanted to think her reluctance to move was due to a boneless contentment that mirrored his. He knew better. She longed to remain cocooned in this small, safe place as much as he longed to keep her here.

Levering himself up on one elbow, he brushed

back her tangled hair. "Worried about what comes next with Claire?"

"Yes."

He responded instinctively to the fear buried in her soft reply. "I'll stay with you, sweetheart. This time, I'll stay."

The endearment just slipped out, but felt so right Drew added a kiss for emphasis. She accepted both with a tremulous smile that got him thinking about delaying their dinner for a little while longer.

Except the smile didn't quite make it to her eyes. Stroking his cheek, she asked again the question he'd been dodging.

"Why are you doing all this for me?"

He almost told her about the *Kallister* then. Probably would have, if she hadn't already had so much to deal with. Instead he gave her half of the truth.

"Did I mention that I'm seriously in lust with you?"

"You did, actually, but I thought we just took care of that problem."

His gaze roamed her sweat-slicked body from the hollow of her throat to the dark hair at the juncture of her thighs. His response this time was one hundred percent true.

"Wrong. All we did was stoke the fire."

He had to kiss her again. That compulsion led to another. His blood stirring, he planed her smooth curves and silk hollows. The muscles of her belly jumped under his palm.

"How hungry are you?" he asked, thinking of the cartons up on deck.

"That depends." Assuming an innocent air, she debated her choices. "Are we talking jade shrimp here? Or hot, spicy beef?"

With a snort of laughter, Drew rolled into her. The answer poked a dent in her hip.

When they finally made it back up on deck, dusk had wrapped the marina in a purple haze. Light spilled from the windows of the restaurants and condos fronting the harbor.

Their shrimp sat in a bucket of congealed white sauce. Drew tossed it over the side to feed the fish and dumped the contents of the unopened cartons on the paper plates. Too hungry to mess with chopsticks, Tracy used a fork to greedily scarf down a healthy portion of beef, noodles, soggy egg rolls and cold tea.

Cleaning up afterward took much less time than she would have preferred. The cartons and paper plates went into a plastic trash sack, to be deposited in the Dumpster at the end of the dock. Drew stowed the table below deck, disconnected the power line from the utility pole on the dock and secured the cabin. Tracy waited on the dock while he snapped the deck cover into place.

Joining her on the dock, he hefted the trash sack. "Ready for phase two with Claire and Mac?"

Dragging in a deep breath, she squared her shoulders. She wasn't real thrilled with the idea of going into a relaxed or near hypnotic state. Her defenses would be down, her mind unguarded. God knew what—or who—might come out.

"Ready as I'll ever be."

Her breezy bravado didn't fool him. Threading his fingers through hers, he squeezed her hand.

"We're in this together, kid."

For now, anyway. Tracy didn't want to think too far into the future. If she did, she'd have to face up to the very distinct possibility she'd never see Drew again after this wild interlude. She'd also have to admit that sometime between crunch-fried fish on Catalina's Green Pier and soggy egg rolls aboard the *Kingfisher*, she'd tumbled into love with the man.

The realization hadn't come on a burst of fireworks. Nor did Tracy know what the heck she was going to do about it. For now, it was enough to hug the knowledge to herself as she and Drew walked the long dock between the slips.

Lights mounted on tall poles dropped splashes of gold on the walkway. The wooden pilings creaked and groaned under their feet. As they neared the end of the dock, she glanced up at the Marina Towers. Half the condos showed brightly lit windows, the other half were dark. Tracy's fingers tightened on Drew's.

He didn't seem to notice. His attention had fixed on a boat just pulling into a slip on a parallel dock.

When he kept it in his view for several paces, Tracy craned her neck to check out the craft.

It was smaller than the *Kingfisher*, but was obviously built for speed. With sleek, long lines, it filled the slip. It's engine was a monster. Wondering why the boat had snagged Drew's interest, Tracy slowed her step to match his.

"Do you know that boat?"

"No. Can you make out her name?"

She squinted into the gathering darkness. "Sorry, it's too far away. Why? What's so interesting about her?"

He watched the boat, his eyes narrowed. "I thought I saw a red blip."

Tracy kept her gaze trained on the craft. A moment later the stern rocked in their direction.

"There. I see it. A steady red glow. That's one of her running lights, isn't it?"

"*That* is."

He observed the craft for another moment or two before ushering Tracy through the gate at the end of the dock.

By the time he'd deposited the trash in the Dumpster and let the lid clank down, she'd forgotten about the speedboat. Reaching instinctively for his hand, she clung to it like a lifeline while they crossed the street and took the elevators to the Marina Towers' twelfth floor.

Chapter 12

Claire and Mac had been busy during their absence. The remains of a pizza littered the coffee table. The MMPI Tracy had completed before she left was once again sealed in the envelope it had come in. The black cases Mackenzie had carried in were stacked against the wall.

The array of equipment those cases had disgorged stopped Tracy in her tracks. Eyes rounding, she dragged her stunned gaze from a laptop bristling with wires to three separate tripod-mounted video cameras to an assortment of devices whose uses she could only guess at.

"What did you do?" she asked the dark-haired

Mackenzie Blair. "Hit a year-end sale at Electronics Are Us?"

Mac looked up from fiddling with one of the cameras and shot her a grin. "Ask anyone who knows me. They'll tell you I firmly believe more is better."

"We don't have to use any of this equipment if it makes you uncomfortable," Claire said calmly.

Tracy shagged a hand through her hair. She now knew how a butterfly must feel at the stealthy approach of a net.

"I'm okay with it."

Mostly.

"Let me clean up and we'll get started."

"Take your time," Claire advised. "Drew arranged for Mac and me to stay in the two-bedroom unit across the hall. We can spend as little or as much time on this project tonight as you wish."

Tracy was tempted. Very tempted. As much as she'd like to spin out her time with Drew McDowell for another day or two or three, however, she wanted to get this over with. She needed Claire to get inside her head and—hopefully!—figure out who was sending these brainwaves.

With another glance at that daunting array of equipment, she made for her bedroom. One quick shower and change later, she returned. She hadn't bothered with makeup or with shoes. The hardwood floor was smooth and cool under her feet, and she swiped her hands down the side seams of her jeans.

Drew had also used the brief interval to comb his hair and clean up. Tracy intercepted the smirk Mackenzie directed his way when he joined them. She said nothing, however, and turned her attention to an instrument that looked like a camera lens angled between two mirrors.

"What's that?" Tracy asked.

"A small-scale version of the multi-spectral thermal imager originally developed by the Department of Energy. It records images in fifteen different spectral bands, ranging from visible to long-wave infrared."

"Ooo-kay."

Grinning, Mackenzie translated for her. "DOE's system is a space-based platform that collects data on everything from the earth's surface temperatures, water quality, cloud movement and vegetation health. This little baby will detect and measure thermal signatures within a fifty-foot radius, depending on where and how I aim it."

"What about the rest of this stuff?"

Mackenzie went around the room, fondling the individual pieces of equipment with the same tenderness a mother might her young children.

"These are electromagnetic field meters. I've triangulated them, as I did the cameras, to cover the entire room. This is a motion detector that utilizes a passive infrared sensor. Here we have the latest in microwave technology."

She launched into a detailed description of what

each device was supposed to measure and record. Tracy's head whirled by the end of the inventory.

"I probably went a little overboard," the brunette admitted sheepishly. "Chalk it up to watching *Ghostbusters* a couple dozen times as a kid."

Her remark triggered two diametrically opposed reactions in Tracy. Part of her wanted to leap with joy at finally hearing someone say the word ghost aloud. The rest of her had to wrestle back a shudder. Setting her jaw, she turned to Claire.

"Let's do this."

"All right. Take a seat."

"Where?"

"Wherever you wish."

Tracy opted for the easy chair and ottoman. Claire chose the sofa. Drew moved to the far corner of the living room, out of sight, while Mackenzie disappeared behind her bank of instruments.

With quiet authority, Claire claimed her client's full attention. "We'll start with some relaxation exercises."

Twenty minutes later, Tracy's head lolled against the back of her chair. Eyes closed, she drifted somewhere between complete bonelessness and sleep.

"What are you thinking?" Claire asked quietly.

"That I haven't felt this relaxed since Uncle Jack's first heart attack."

"Tell me about him."

"He was so good to me. He lived right next door and would look after me when my aunt had to work."

Memories floated through her head like wisps of clouds. Soft and downy, they filled Tracy with a warm joy as she shared them with Claire. She could almost feel Jack's thorny palm grasping her hand when he walked her to the first day of second grade. Her senses tingled with the delicious anticipation that used to shiver through her before her first lick of the ice-cream cones he'd buy her. Her mouth curving, she related her prom date's nervousness when she took him next door to stand inspection.

Claire said little, content to let Tracy's memories carry her where they would. Mac stayed out of view but kept busy with her various instruments. Drew likewise remained in the background. Arms crossed, he leaned a shoulder against the wall and fought the guilt that needled through him.

Although he'd been the one to suggest Tracy talk to a professional, he was just beginning to appreciate the courage it took for her to lay herself open to complete strangers, with a battery of digital cameras recording every word. She'd taken Claire on trust. Mac, as well. Because Drew had vouched for them. Now she was letting them all inside her head, again because he'd asked it of her.

He felt like a damned voyeur.

Wrenching his gaze from the dark head just visible above the high seatback, he scowled at the panorama outside the wall-to-wall windows. Floodlit palms dotted the grounds far below. Across the street the restaurants and shops fronting the marina did a brisk business. Lights winked amid the forest of masts and antennas sprouting from the slips.

Drew angled his stance and counted the slips. The speedboat was still there, a faint white blur in the darkness. The red blip he'd spotted emanating from the boat a while ago preyed on his mind.

The pulse of light had come and gone so quickly. He'd thought at first it had originated from inside the cabin, an emission put out by the boat's navigational equipment or some other electronic device. Drew probably wouldn't have given it a second thought if the short, quick pulse hadn't lanced through the night like a sword.

Or the beam of a rifle's laser sight.

Drew couldn't have survived all these years working for OMEGA without a healthy dose of paranoia. Every operative hauled a lot of baggage into the field with him, including a prickling sixth sense that warned of danger lurking behind every bush. His was working overtime right now.

He'd go back down to the dock, he decided. Check out the speedboat. As soon as Claire finished with Tracy. He didn't want to interrupt their dialogue, particularly with Tracy's memories giving way to less comforting ones. He swung his glance her way and winced at the raw pain that had crept into her voice.

"It hurt so much to watch him growing weaker every day."

"How long was he ill?" Claire asked gently.

"Three years off and on. He broke his hip in a fall and had to have it replaced. He did fine for a while, until he had his first heart attack."

Her breath left on a sigh.

"Congestive heart failure. That's what the cardiologists termed it. They put in stents after the first attack, a defibrillator after the second. The rehab took longer each time."

Her head was still propped against the chair back. Her eyes remained closed. But she was anything but relaxed now as she relived the long months of anguish.

"He lost so much weight. I cooked all his meals, every dish he'd once loved. I even tried to bribe him into eating. He got so weak and thin they finally put in a feeding tube."

Drew had to steel himself against her quiet anguish. He wouldn't help her by busting into the session and cradling her in his arms.

"Watching him dwindle down to skin and bones was almost more than I could bear. He used to be so big and strong and full of life. And handsome," she added on another sigh. "I remember seeing pictures of him in uniform. He was a real hunk."

Claire caught Drew's eye. She'd been briefed on his mission and knew he had yet to determine exactly how the *Kallister* fit into the triangle that included

Tracy, her adopted uncle and Trixie Halston. After a swift inner debate, Claire decided she wouldn't violate professional ethics if she followed the thread Tracy had thrown out.

"Jack wore a uniform?"

"He served in World War Two. In the merchant marines." A small crease appeared between her eyebrows. "Only he didn't go by Jack then."

A small movement across the room brought Claire's head up. Uncrossing his arms, Drew pushed away from the wall he'd been leaning against. His frown mirrored Tracy's.

Feeling her way cautiously now, Claire returned her attention to the woman across from her. "You say your uncle didn't go by Jack?"

The slash between her eyebrows deepened. Her hands curled on the arms of her chair.

"Johnny. They called him Johnny."

"Who did?"

"His shipmates." The reply came in a voice she seemed to pull from deep inside. "Kenny, Ed, me, the whole orchestra. We all called him Johnny."

Drew took an involuntary step forward but stepped back when Claire shot him a warning glance.

"I'm confused. Who are you referring to when you say 'we'?"

Tracy's lids lifted. Irritation and the beginnings of anger glittered in her eyes. "I just told you. Kenny. Ed. Me. The sidemen. All of us."

Mackenzie went perfectly still behind her array of instruments. Drew didn't so much as breathe. A thin, brittle silence enveloped the entire room.

"I'm sorry, but I still don't understand. You'll have to explain, Tracy. Tell me who—"

"Tracy? Jesus!"

Claire managed not to jump when the woman seated across from her flung herself out of her chair. Barely. The move was so abrupt and so violent it seemed to create a kind of swirling vortex. Claire could swear she heard the pictures on the wall rattle.

"Why do I have to go through this every time?" Tracy raged. "Why doesn't anyone believe me?"

She whirled, spotted Drew and locked on him like a sidewinder missile.

"Tell them!"

The force of her demand pulled him in, made him part of the circle. Still, Drew waited for Claire's nod before responding to the imperious command.

"Tell them what?"

"Who I am."

"I've got a good idea," he said carefully, "but it might be better coming from you."

"Oh, for crissakes!" Thoroughly disgusted, she spun back to Claire. "The name's Trixie. Trixie Halston. Which Drew would admit if he weren't so damned stubborn. Or hadn't just been bumping gums and grinding hips with little Miss Tracy," she added spitefully.

"I see."

The calm reply elicited a sneer.

"What? What do you see? Or should I say, who do you see? No answer? Still don't want to believe me? Okay, I'll make it easy for you. Drew, baby, turn on the music. The canary wants to sing."

When he didn't move, she threw a look over her shoulder so malicious he felt its impact where he stood.

"Turn on the music."

Every inch of his skin tightened. His spine crawling, he looked to Claire. This was her show, although she seemed to share his sense that it was fast spinning out of control. She took several seconds longer to dip her head this time.

The CD Tracy had made in Catalina was still in the tray. When Drew hit Play, he was asked to select a track. He punched one in at random. A few seconds later, the Kenny Jones Orchestra flowed into the introductory bars of a melody Drew now knew by heart.

"Oh, baby!" Tracy…Trixie…whoever!…whooped with delight. "You chose my song."

She began to sway in time to the smooth, mellow strains of the same tune they'd listened to repeatedly for the past few days and nights. Drew wasn't surprised when she joined in on the vocal, but could see both Claire and Mac blink in astonishment at her perfect harmony with the smoky-voiced contralto.

Last time she'd sung the song through to the end

before tears began to slide down her cheeks. Tonight, she made it only to the second chorus before the words thickened and gradually choked off.

"Damn him," she whispered hoarsely as the band picked up the refrain. "I had a career. A future. Everyone said so. Kenny. Ed. I hope Johnny's burning in hell."

Her grief was so raw and so real that Drew started toward her. Claire stopped him.

"Don't you know whether or not he's burning?" she asked with the same cool detachment she might use when asking directions to the nearest park. "You heard Tracy describe his death, saw her scatter his ashes. You must know he's passed on."

"Of course I do! Why do you think I came back?"

"I don't know. Tell me."

"*Because* the bastard passed on!"

She began to pace, her movements jerky and out of rhythm with the last strains of the song.

"Johnny was meant to die. It was his time. But it wasn't mine. All those years ago... I wasn't supposed to die. Not then. Not in such a horrible way. And I didn't know what would come next. How could I know?"

"What did come next, Tracy?"

"Trixie, dammit! Trixie."

The near shriek pinged off the walls, high and shrill and laced with fury. Mackenzie dropped into an instinctive crouch. Drew caught himself wishing he were armed and spit out a low curse. Claire hung on to her equanimity with an obvious effort.

"All right. What came next, Trixie?"

"I was just… Just…"

She cut small, vicious circles in the air with one hand, looking for the right phrase, pulling it from the dark reaches of her mind.

"Just drifting in a sort of emptiness until little Miss Tracy brought him back to Catalina." Anguish cut through her rage. "That's where we met, Johnny and me. That's where he killed me."

As if to punctuate her roiling emotions, the music ended with a sad, haunting flourish. Thunderous applause followed, but none of the four caught up in the unfolding drama spared a thought for the thousands of dancers who waited eagerly for the next song.

Drew was the first to move. With a muttered curse, he reached for the switch to cut off the CD, as he had last night. The husky voice that spilled from the speakers halted his hand in midair.

"Good night to all you mariners. Stay safe."

"Hey!" The would-be Trixie spun toward the entertainment center. "That's my sign-off."

"*And to all you men of the SS* Kallister, *keep a song in your heart.*"

"The *Kallister*," she wailed. Fury once again suffused her face. Hands bunched into fists, she faced Drew. "Did you hear that?"

Hell, yes, he'd heard it.

Like the flashing squares of a Rubik's Cube, the brightly colored pieces swirled in his mind. They had to fit together. The bloodstained note they'd found in Trixie's pocket. This seemingly casual mention of the *Kallister* on a radio broadcast beamed across the nation. The torpedo that ripped through the ship's hull.

Suspicion grabbed him by the throat and wouldn't let go. He kept it out of his voice by a sheer force of will.

"Why did you mention that particular ship in your sign-off, Trixie?"

"That was Johnny's ship! I'd heard he was leaving soon. I was afraid I'd never see him again. I wanted him to know I'd wait for him."

Her anger lashed at Drew, much as it had at Nick's, and propelled her across the room.

"That night. At the Avalon Casino. I was going to tell him I'd marry him. The next day, if he could arrange it. The *next* day!"

They stood toe-to-toe now. The marina where Drew had buried himself in Tracy's hot, welcoming flesh such a short time ago was clearly visible in the wall-to-wall windows. It might have been light years away, along with the woman who'd triggered Drew's protective instincts.

He tried. He really tried. But he couldn't dredge up a single urge to protect or shield or comfort this raging female. The only switches she tripped were distrust and suspicion and a sudden, chilling unease.

The explanation for that chill hit him like a steel pipe to the back of the head. She wasn't Tracy. She didn't come anywhere close to Tracy.

Drew barely had time to register that wild thought before a faint, pulsing red beam entered his field of view. It came from outside the windows, slicing upward at a sharp angle. He followed it for a second, maybe two, before it centered on the temple of the woman facing him.

Drew didn't take time to think. Didn't shout a warning. Swinging his arm, he batted her away at the same instant the wall-to-wall windows shattered, showering them both in glass shards.

Chapter 13

The crack of shattering glass was still reverberating through the condo when the three OMEGA operatives exploded into action.

Drew lunged for the target, covering her with his body. Mac dropped like a stone and slithered on her belly toward the black leather carrying cases stacked in the foyer. Cyrene dove for her purse. Ripping out a 9mm Walther PPK, she hit the floor next to Drew.

"What the hell was that?"

"Sniper."

His gut a tight ball of fear, he jerked to the side and rolled Tracy over. The shooter had painted her. In that frozen heartbeat before Drew swatted her out of the way, the bastard had pulled the trigger. Drew knew all too well the kind of damage a sniper bullet did to a human skull.

To his everlasting relief, there was no blood, no gore, no splatter of brain or bone. Only shocked green eyes staring at him in disbelief.

"What...? Who...?"

He didn't have time for explanations.

"Stay down! Cyrene, cover her."

He rolled up and into a low crouch. Broken glass crunched under his feet as he raced for the bedroom. Cursing himself for leaving his weapon in his suitcase, he yanked the Glock from its hidden compartment, slapped in a magazine and hit the door.

"Call 911," he barked to Cyrene on the run. "And watch for uninvited visitors. The sniper might have someone in the building, waiting to verify the kill."

"Roger that."

Mackenzie had gained the protective shelter of the foyer and ripped open one of the black leather cases. With swift efficiency, she chambered a round in a snub-nosed .38.

"I've got your back, Riev."

Mac hadn't trained as a field agent, but Drew had witnessed her skill at the firing range. She could put six rounds dead center. Drew suspected Lightning wouldn't be thrilled to learn his wife had gone after a sniper, but he'd worry about his boss's reaction later. Right now he was more than happy to have Mac as backup.

Yanking open the door, he dropped into another crouch and swept the hall before sprinting for the stairs. This wasn't the time to wait for elevators. Mac slammed the condo door and raced after him.

"Did you get an angle on the shooter?" she asked as they pounded down eleven flights of stairs.

"He fired from the marina across the street."

Drew flew around the eighth-floor landing.

"White speedboat."

The seventh floor passed in a blur.

"Second row of slips."

His longer legs gave him a substantial lead over Mac. She lagged one flight behind when he gained the fourth floor, two flights by the time he slammed through the emergency exit at the bottom of the stairs.

The alarm went off, emitting a shriek that followed Drew across the palm-dotted grounds. Dodging traffic, he charged across the wide boulevard fronting the marina and through the alley between two restaurants.

He spotted the speedboat as soon as he hit the concrete walkway that stretched the length of the docks. Churning a white wake at its stern, the high-speed craft was backing out of its slip.

Cursing, Drew skidded to a stop. He'd never reach the damned thing before it cleared the slip, reversed engines and aimed for the mouth of the stone breakwater.

But he *could* reach the *Kingfisher*. The speedboat had to cut within twenty yards of Charlie's boat to make that narrow mouth.

Whirling, Drew tore down the dock he and Tracy had ambled along such a short time ago. Concrete gave way to wood. The finger piers between the slips flashed by. Utility pole after utility pole fell behind him.

The speedboat came up on his left, fifty yards out. Drew put on another burst of speed. Lungs pumping, he kept up with the boat as it angled toward the opening in the breakwater.

The separation between the end of the dock and the speedboat shrank to forty yards. Thirty.

Drew saw a shadow pass in front of a navigational screen, blocking its green glow. The bastard at the wheel was in black, he realized. Head-to-toe. Watch cap. Wet suit. Face paint. He'd taken no chances.

Drew couldn't see the sniper, but he knew damned well the shooter could see him. The spots mounted on tall poles at regular intervals bathed him in light as he raced to intercept the speeding craft. They also illuminated the Glock .45 law enforcement special. The weapon was designed for lethal force, not concealment.

The *Kingfisher*'s slip lay dead ahead. Suddenly, a pulsing red beam shot across the water.

Drew swerved left. The beam cut with him.

A waist-high utility pole less than a foot away burst into a shower of sparks.

No report. No muzzle flash. This guy knew his business.

When a red dot speared into his chest, Drew dived for the dock. He didn't hear the second shot whiz over his head, but he sure as hell felt its percussive force. The Glock bucking in his hands, he returned fire.

His first shot cracked one of the speedboat's metal deck struts. His second shattered the navigational screen and extinguished its green glow. Drew pumped out a third just as a bullet gouged into the dock mere inches from his face. A splinter blazed a fiery trail along one eyebrow, missing his eye by millimeters. He was blinking away the blood when the speedboat exploded.

His ears ringing from the blast, Drew watched the dark sea just inside the breakwater blossom into a fireball. Waves of heat rolled through the night. Debris and burning fuel rained down, hissing and spitting when they hit the water.

The pieces were still coming down when Mackenzie dropped to her haunches beside him. "Did you take a hit, Riev?"

"Only from a piece of the dock."

Pushing upright, he swiped at the blood with his sleeve. Mac sat on her heels beside him and watched the show while Drew unclipped his cell phone. A two-digit code connected him directly with Cyrene.

"What's the situation there?" he bit out.

"We're secure. No uninvited visitors. How about you two?"

"We're okay."

"I take it that red glow lighting the sky is our shooter."

"What's left of him."

Sirens wailed in the distance. Drew dragged his sleeve across his forehead again. His mind had already leaped ahead to the barrage of questions he'd have to answer.

"The locals are about to arrive. Mac and I will handle things at this end. Contact OMEGA Control and advise Denise of the situation."

"Will do, Riever."

Tracy faced Claire across the small table they'd dragged into a corner, well away from the shattered window. The massive entertainment center formed a protective barrier on one side. The coffee table they'd toppled onto its side shielded them on the other. The terror she'd choked back for five terrifying minutes threatened to suffocate her.

"Was that Drew? Please tell me that was Drew!"

"It was. He and Mac are okay."

Still numb with shock, she tried to interpret Claire's one-sided conversation. It didn't make any more sense than the semiautomatic the slender blonde handled with such cool authority.

"Why did you call him Riever?"

Claire flashed her a quick look. Barely a strand of her pale hair was out of place. Tracy, on the other hand, was fast coming apart at the seams.

"Tell me, Claire! Who are you? Who is this person you call Riever?"

After a brief hesitation, the psychologist appeared to reach an internal decision. If she *was* a psychologist. After seeing her leap into action, Tracy wouldn't have put money on it.

"Riever is Drew's code name. Mine is Cyrene. He and Mac and I work for a government agency. Drew will explain when he gets here. In the meantime, I have to make another call. Stay put and I'll…"

"No!" Snagging the blonde's blouse, Tracy spun her around. "I want answers. Now!"

Claire or Cyrene or whoever the hell she was directed a pointed glance at her bunched sleeve. When she lifted her head, ice coated her voice.

"I need to make this call, Tracy. It's important."

"One call. Then we talk."

"One call. Then I tell you as much as I can without preempting Riever. He wouldn't appreciate that."

"Tough noogies."

"Noogies?" The ice cracked. A smile slipped through. "Is that the best you can do after all this?"

Her graceful gesture encompassed the overturned furniture, the gaping hole in the window and glittering glass shards scattered across the parquet floor.

"I'll work on something more appropriate while you make your call," Tracy muttered.

She'd also work on stitching her frayed nerves back together. Sinking into her chair, she locked her hands together to forestall a return of the shakes.

Deliberately lowering her defenses so a long-dead singer could pour out her rage and anguish had come close to ripping Tracy apart. The possibility a sniper had targeted her pretty well completed the job.

Why in God's name would anyone target her? Claire had to be mistaken. Maybe *she* was the intended victim. Or Mac. Incredible as it sounded, both women apparently led double lives. So did Drew.

Tracy's grip went so tight her nails dug furrows in the backs of her hands. What a fool she'd been! What a stupid, trusting, naive fool! Like some brainless twit, she'd accepted Drew McDowell's sudden appearance in her life, let him shrug aside her questions and allowed him into her head.

And her heart, she acknowledged, cringing inside. After so many years of holding out for Mr. Right, she'd fallen for a smooth, sexy liar.

Way to go, Brandt! Way to go.

"All right, Tracy." Claire slid into the chair she'd positioned against the wall. "I've made my call. Fire when ready."

"First question. Are you really a psychologist?"

"Yes, I am. I'm licensed to practice in three states.

I've also recently been licensed in Mexico, where my husband and I maintain a residence. I'll be happy to provide you with my credentials, if you wish."

A two-ton boulder rolled off Tracy's back. At least she hadn't let some pseudoshrink muck around in her psyche.

Now for the big one.

"What about Drew? Does he know a '57 Chevy from a snowmobile?"

"According to my husband, Drew McDowell can take anything on four wheels apart and put it back together in his sleep." Smiling, Claire fondled the square-cut rock on her ring finger. "I might add that Luis is presently cruising through the Sonora Desert at what I would conservatively guess is about one hundred and ten miles per hour, compliments of his best bud, Drew. Next question?"

"Mackenzie Blair. Is that her real name?"

"It is, although she usually uses a hyphen in social situations. Her married name is Mackenzie Blair-Jensen. Her husband is Nick Jensen."

"The same Nick who owns Nick's?"

"Yes."

With sickening clarity, the pieces of the puzzle fell into place. Drew's connections. His high-priced condo. The standing reservations at one of the world's most expensive restaurant chains. His flexible schedule and offer to aid her in her quest.

"It was all a setup," Tracy whispered raggedly.

"Right from the start. Drew—Riever—didn't just suddenly drop into my life. He targeted me, too."

"Yes, he did."

"Why?"

"He'll have to answer that one. You're *his* op."

"Op?"

"Operation. Mission." Claire spread her hands. "Assignment."

"Assignment. Right."

The psychologist hesitated, no doubt searching for a middle ground between what she should and what she wanted to say.

"If it helps at all, I can tell you I've worked with Riever for going on six years now. As far as I know, he's never bumped gums or ground hips with a target before."

Tracy's mouth curled in distaste. "Is that how he described it? Bumping gums and grinding hips?"

"That's how *you* described it."

The boulder that had rolled off her back just moments ago slammed into her again, hitting square between the shoulder blades. She hadn't uttered those crude phrases. Trixie had, using her as a mouthpiece. But Claire obviously didn't believe that. Feeling suddenly, inexplicably weary, Tracy abandoned the field of battle.

"Maybe you're right. Maybe I should hold the rest of my questions for Drew."

"I think that's wise."

* * *

It was well past 10:00 p.m. when Drew finally made it back to the condo. In addition to Mac, he had Detective Dan Riley, his partner, and a crime-scene unit in tow.

One of the EMTs who'd responded to the scene had cleansed the cut above his eye and closed it with a butterfly bandage. Drew had swiped the blood off his face and neck with wet wipes, but the stains on his shirt made Tracy gasp and Claire ask sharply, "What happened?"

"I got in the way of a flying splinter."

After introducing Claire, Drew took the detectives and evidence techs into the living room to search for the bullet fired by the sniper. It didn't require much looking to find the hole it had burrowed into the ceiling. Using long, narrow forceps, the techs extracted the spent bullet and dropped it into a plastic evidence bag.

"Looks like a .fifty-cal Whisper," the tech advised Riley. "Same as the one we dug out of the wharf. Heavy, pointed, low drag. Specially designed for high-powered rifles fitted with silencers."

"Looks like," Riley agreed, his expression thoughtful under the splotchy purple birthmark. His gaze shifted to Drew. "We don't see many Whispers in our nightly round of drive-bys and street shootings."

"This wasn't a drive-by or a street shooting. This was a professional hit."

"That's what it's sounding like to us, too. Guess we'd better talk to Miss Brandt and see if she knows why someone wants to take her out."

Miss Brandt didn't have a clue. Battling a sick feeling in the pit of her stomach, Tracy doggedly answered the detectives' questions.

"I don't have any enemies. None that I know of, anyway."

"What about your family? Could someone have a grudge against one of them?"

"My neighbor—Jack Foster—was the closest thing I had to family, but he died a few weeks ago."

"Are you a beneficiary in his will?"

"He didn't have one."

"So who inherits his estate?"

"There is no estate. Everything Jack owned went to pay his medical bills."

Along with most of what Tracy owned. Forcing back the memories of her friend's last, painful months, she put a few questions of her own to Riley.

"Why are you so sure I was the target?"

"We're not sure of anything at this point, but Drew—Mr. McDowell—said he saw you painted with a red laser beam the instant before the windows shattered."

If that were true, Tracy ought to feel nothing but grateful to Drew for knocking her aside and saving her life. Gratitude was having a tough time cutting through her anger and hurt at learning she was his *assignment*.

"Drew and I were standing next to each other. Not more than a foot apart. Maybe I just got in the way. Maybe he was the target."

As hard as she tried to hold it in, the anger seeped out. She looked past the detectives and pinned Drew with a cold stare.

"Why don't you ask Mr. McDowell who he works for? Who *his* enemies are?"

The icy zinger took Drew by surprise. Stiffening, he shot Cyrene a quick look. His fellow operative dipped her head in a small nod.

Well, hell!

Drew had figured he'd have to do some serious explaining after the detectives departed the condo. Tracy had seen him bolt out of there with his Glock. She'd also witnessed Cyrene and Mac in action. She had to know then they weren't exactly who they'd purported to be.

"Mr. McDowell has already apprised us of his government connections," Riley said stiffly.

The LAPD detective wasn't real happy about being left in the dark for so long, either. He'd made Drew well aware of his feelings down on the dock.

"We're working with him on his end of things," Riley finished. "Maybe we'll uncover some leads when the lab sifts through the debris recovered from the marina. With any luck, our divers will also recover some remains. We might be able to run the shooter's DNA."

The comment wrenched Drew's thoughts from a newly deceased sniper to a long-dead singer.

"Speaking of DNA, were your lab folks able to lift any from the note in Trixie Halston's pocket?"

"No. Sorry. But we did get a hit on the prints. I was going to call you tomorrow." Dragging a black notebook from his hip pocket, he flipped through the pages. "Halston's prints were all over the note, as I told you at the station. The other set checked to an old geezer named LaSorta."

"Ed LaSorta?"

"You know him?"

"He used to do PR for the same band Halston sang with. We talked to him yesterday morning, before we came to see you. How did his prints get in the system?"

"Cops busted him at some Hollywood party way back in the sixties, along with a half dozen others, and charged him with possession. They were after the dealer, so LaSorta got off with a slap on the knuckles. First-time offense, negligible amount, you know how it goes."

"Yeah," Drew said slowly, "I know how it goes."

Except this case wasn't going anywhere that made sense. What was LaSorta's connection to the *Kallister?* Why had Trixie specifically referenced that ship in her sign-off?

The same suspicion that had reared its ugly head while he'd listened to Trixie earlier grabbed him by the throat again. Drew would have to pay LaSorta another visit and find out just what the man knew about the *Kallister,* then and now.

First he had to stash Tracy in a safe house and make sure she stayed there until he figured out who the hell had targeted her and why.

Chapter 14

By the time Detective Riley and the others left,
Tracy was feeling the effects of the long, nerve-
bending day. Terror and tension had drained her of
every drop of energy. A headache throbbed at the
base of her skull. Her bruised wrist smarted every
time she bent it.

Her bruised pride hurt far worse. Wrapped in
stony silence, she packed her things. The condo was
uninhabitable. More to the point, Drew didn't
consider it safe. He'd arranged for them all to move
to another location and wanted to make the transition
immediately.

The three of them were waiting in the foyer when

Tracy rolled out her bag. Mac had her equipment in cases that stacked neatly on a fold-up dolly. Claire's weekender sat beside her leather pumps. Drew had changed his bloodstained shirt and windbreaker for a sky-blue crewneck sweater.

"I need you and Mac to switch jackets," he told Tracy. "Her coloring's the same as yours. In that pea-green windbreaker, she can pass easily for you."

And just when she'd convinced herself she was too numb to feel another jolt of fear! She swiped her tongue over suddenly dry lips.

"Do you really think they might try again?"

Whoever "they" were.

"I didn't think they would try the first time," he said in a tone riddled with self-disgust. "No sense taking more chances until we figure this thing out. Mac, you'll ride with me in the Mustang. Tracy, you'll ride in the back seat of Claire's rental. I want you to stay low and out of sight until we get where we're going."

"Where *are* we going?"

"A bungalow in the hills above L.A. It belongs to a friend of a friend, who's out of town at the moment."

"Convenient."

"Yes, it is."

"We need to talk about these friends of yours."

"We will. Let's get you moved first."

He'd done it again, she realized as she scrunched down in the back seat of Claire's rental. Damned if he hadn't palmed her off with another "we'll talk later." Tracy was almost as tired of Drew McDowell's slick evasions as Trixie Halston's intrusive visits.

Her iron determination to squeeze the truth out of him barely survived the trip to their new quarters, however. The drive was short, probably not more than twenty minutes, but the throbbing at the base of Tracy's skull increased in tempo and ferocity with each mile.

So did her exhaustion. No surprise there, considering how she'd bared her soul to a shrink, made passionate love, played host to a vindictive ghost and dodged a bullet, all within the space of five or six hours.

As a consequence, she could barely put one foot in front of the other when Drew helped her out of the back seat and carried her bag into the two-story house he'd euphemistically termed a bungalow.

The women claimed the three bedrooms upstairs. Drew dumped his gear in the downstairs den before delivering Tracy's bag to her room. It was done in a blend of California modern and wine country rustic, with a corner fireplace, arched doorways and Saltillo tile accents and a king-size four-poster bed draped in airy gauze.

Drew could hardly avoid the bed when he set her bag on the floor. It stretched between them, as wide as the Pacific, and raised several questions in Tracy's tired mind, not the least of which was whether he would have the nerve to suggest they share it.

He must have gotten the message back at the condo.

He made no reference at all to sleeping arrangements, merely advising her he'd wait downstairs.

"We can talk tonight or in the morning. Your call."

"Will you be here in the morning?" Acid dripped through the polite query. "The government won't require your presence elsewhere?"

"I'll be here. I told you earlier this evening, I'm staying with you."

"It's what you didn't tell me that hurts."

"Yeah, I know."

He paused beside her. The butterfly bandage showed white against his eyebrow, reminding Tracy that he'd faced down the sniper. The stark reminder took some of the sting from his deception.

Not all of it, though. Enough remained to send her back a step when he reached out to brush a knuckle down her cheek.

His hand dropped. Regret flickered across his face. "I'll be downstairs."

It took her a while to pull herself together. Her first order of business was to slap some water on her face and drag a brush through her hair. The bristles dislodged several glass slivers that tinkled into the sink. Like Drew's bandage, those glittering shards were a harsh reminder of how close they'd both come to disaster.

Her hand shaking, she turned the faucet to full blast and washed the slivers down the drain. Since she'd run out of underwear and outerwear, she took a few minutes to rinse several pairs of panties and her fuzzy green sweater. Hopefully, it would dry before morning.

A murmur of voices drifted from the den when Tracy went downstairs. Claire was there with Drew. She'd released her hair from its neat coil. The silky stream spilled down her back in a way that made her look five years younger and far more approachable. The jeans and Penn State sweatshirt she'd changed into took off another five years.

"Here's Tracy now." She smiled a welcome. "How are you holding up?"

"By a very thin thread."

"I'm not surprised. It's been a rather eventful day." With that masterful understatement, she scooped up the wineglass on the table beside her chair and rose. "I need to call my husband and I know you want to talk to Drew, so I'll leave you two alone."

Like the upstairs rooms, the den combined modern utility with touches of California's past. Built-in oak cabinets housed an entertainment center, wet bar and extensive wine collection. Framed posters of western movies starring a young John Wayne and a six-gun-toting Tom Mix decorated the walls. A black-and-white cowhide throw was draped over the back of a sofa with chrome arms and legs.

"Would you like a glass of wine? Claire says it's a very good Merlot."

"No, thanks. I'm so tired one glass would put me out for the count. Where's Mackenzie?"

"Upstairs, fiddling with her instruments. She's hoping her handy-dandy spectrometer recorded the thermal signature of the red beam."

"And if it did? What will that tell us?"

"It could give us a clue as to the type of laser sight the shooter used. All we have right now are the two bullets we dug out of the dock and ceiling of the condo. I'm not real hopeful the rifle or the scope survived the speedboat's explosion or that the LAPD divers with be able to find them. If not, we'll need more than those two bullets to ID the bastard."

"Who's *we*, Drew? Who do you and Claire and Mac really work for?"

"A very small and very secret government agency that reports directly to the president. It's a full-time job for Mac. Claire and I are activated only when our services are needed."

Good Lord! It sounded like something right out of a spy novel. Tracy could see Drew in the role of James Bond. And either of his female counterparts could teach Pussy Galore a trick or two. She just couldn't figure out where she fit in to the picture.

"Go on."

Sinking onto the smooth, hairy black-and-white throw, she waited with exaggerated patience for him to proceed.

"You're not going to like what comes next," he warned.

"Go on."

"We received intelligence that someone had initiated a series of queries about a U.S. navy ship transporting a highly classified cargo."

"Me checking out the *Kallister?*"

"Correct."

"But I told you why I was interested in her! Because of Jack and Trixie Halston. I was looking for information from 1941."

"We didn't know that at the time I was activated. All we had to go on was that you'd lost your job with a defense contractor. And that you'd told your former boss he'd be sorry for firing you."

"Because I'd covered his ass more times than he ever knew!"

"That's your take. He put a different slant on it. When you started poking around, trying to ferret out information about a U.S. naval vessel hauling a very sensitive cargo, we had to check you out."

His meaning hit her like a slap to the face. Incredulous, she sprang off the cowhide.

"Wait a minute! Are you saying you thought I might have a grudge against the government, in the form of my ex-boss? That I might leak or sell or otherwise compromise sensitive information about a U.S. naval vessel?"

"I'm saying those were distinct possibilities. In today's climate, we have to follow every thread."

She was so stunned she couldn't breathe. Learning that she was Drew's "assignment" had angered and hurt her. Hearing *why* he'd been instructed to get up close and personal with her sucked every ounce of air from her lungs.

Devastated, Tracy flashed back to the moments they'd shared these past few days. Sitting shoulder to shoulder on the Green Pier. Watching that glorious sunset the first night at the Marina Del Ray. Spending the night with her head cradled on his lap. Writhing and moaning as he took her to a shattering climax aboard the *Kingfisher*.

Oh, God!

She didn't try to hide her humiliation or disgust. Eyes flashing, she raked him with withering scorn.

"That's some job you have, McDowell. The government pays you to wine and dine suspects at the finest restaurants. You get to live the good life while you play on their fears and insecurities. All the while, you're screwing them. Literally and figuratively."

Drew had known this moment would come. He'd braced himself for Tracy's contempt and anger. Being prepared for both didn't make them go down any easier.

"The government isn't paying me to screw you, Tracy. Literally *or* figuratively."

"Oh, I see." Her lip curled. "You just decided to have a little fun on the side while you did your duty."

She'd nailed him with that one. Drew had no defense but the truth.

"Yes, I did."

She hadn't expected him to own up to it. Momentarily speechless, she gaped at him. Drew figured he had all of five seconds to plead his case before she recovered from her surprise and let him have it with both barrels.

"I broke all the rules there on the *Kingfisher*. Problem is, I couldn't help myself. My hunger for you got away from me."

"Ha!"

"I put you ahead of my mission. That's never happened before, Tracy. Ever."

She wasn't buying it. Contempt in every line of her rigid body, she looked down her nose at him. No small feat, considering their differences in height.

"And I should believe you because…?"

"Because it's true."

"Come on, McDowell. After all your lies and deceit, you'll have to do better than that."

"I haven't lied to you. Not once."

"Oh, no? What about all these so-called 'friends' of yours? Convenient how they just pop up when you need them."

"Mac and Claire *are* my friends. So are the other operatives I work with."

"And the condo at Marina Del Ray? The *Kingfisher*? I'm sure you can really afford those."

"As a matter of fact, I can."

He could see her searching her memory bank, scrambling for something to hit him with. She came up with a good one.

"Let's talk about your promise to help me exorcise the ghost of Trixie Halston. What was that, if not a lie?"

"Best I recall, I promised to help you solve the puzzle of her death."

"No, Drew. You said...or at least implied...that you believed me when I said Trixie was inside me, clawing to get out. You said you'd felt her anger, that night at the restaurant. You *talked* to her just a while ago, right before that bullet came through the window. I heard you, Drew. You asked her about the *Kallister.*"

"Jesus, Tracy! I've been a little busy since that bullet came through the window. I haven't had time to think about what happened right before."

She refused to let him off the hook. "Think about it now. I want a straight answer. No evasions. No lies. Who were you pumping for information? Trixie, or me?"

Drew managed not to squirm, but it took a conscious effort of will. Every rational corner of his mind resisted the notion of a ghost. Yet he couldn't deny that instant of irrational certainty earlier. For the space of a single heartbeat he'd stood toe-to-toe with a raging female and known somewhere deep inside that she wasn't Tracy.

Wrapping a hand around the back of his neck, Drew made an unenthusiastic, unwilling leap of faith. "Okay, here's as straight an answer as I can give you. My head says that was you. My gut says otherwise."

"Go with your gut, Drew." Her plea spiraled into a near sob. *"Please!"*

If he'd needed any more evidence of how this business with the dead singer was ripping her apart, she'd just handed it to him. He found himself wishing with every fiber of his being he could reach inside her, grab Trixie Halston by the throat and tear the singer out.

He also wished to hell he'd never seen the movie *The Exorcist*. Shoving images of Linda Blair's blood-red eyes and cracked skin out of his head, he folded Tracy into his arms.

She came reluctantly, still angry with him but needing the comfort of human contact as much as he needed to give it. Drew nuzzled her temple with his chin and wondered if Claire could give them a couple's discount.

Tracy was still in his arms when Mackenzie burst into the den a few moments later, waving the plastic case of a CD.

"You guys aren't going to believe this!" Her face ablaze with excitement, she threw a quick glance around the room. "Where's Claire?"

"Upstairs. She said she had to call Luis. Why?"

"She needs to be here for this."

"For what? What have you got, Mac?"

Instead of answering, she dashed into the hall and bellowed up the stairs. "Cyrene! We need you down here! On the double, girl."

While she waited for Claire to make an appearance, Mac rapped out orders to Drew and Tracy like a drill sergeant on speed.

"You two. Sit. Over there, in front of the TV. Leave a spot for Claire. Oh, good! Here you are. Sit over there next to Drew and Tracy."

Lifting an eyebrow, the third member of their team did as directed. "What's going on?"

"Beats me," Drew replied. "This is Mac's show."

Grabbing the universal remote, the brunette aimed it at the TV and stabbed buttons until a picture popped onto the screen. Another stab switched the input from cable to DVD.

"I haven't had time to clean this up," she warned, inserting the disk. "You'll be watching raw footage from three different feeds. I spliced it together and copied it to disk, but some of the transitions are rough."

The screen fuzzed, then sharpened. A high-intensity image of the living room of the Marina Del Ray condo filled the wide screen. Centered in the screen was Tracy.

She occupied the overstuffed easy chair. She had her feet propped on the footstool and her head resting against the high-backed chair. The camera had captured her at an angle, giving a clear view of her profile.

"What are you thinking?"

Claire's voice came from off-screen. Eyes closed, Tracy murmured a response.

"That I haven't felt this relaxed since Uncle Jack's first heart attack."

"Tell me about him."

With a little jerk, the camera angle switched to a frontal shot. Drew's chest tightened at the quiet grief that etched itself into Tracy's face. Watching this had to be as tough on her as going through it.

"He was so good to me. He lived right next door."

The video played on, switching angles as Tracy followed Claire's gentle prompts and shared her most precious memories. Drew had felt like a voyeur the first time he'd listened to their dialogue. Hearing it again, watching her through the dispassionate eye of a video camera, magnified those feelings a hundred times.

He kept silent, knowing Mac wouldn't put Tracy through another public display without a reason. Certain Mac had caught the red laser beam on video, he leaned forward and watched the screen intently. Just moments later he discovered it was what Mac *hadn't* caught that had her so excited.

"Here it comes," she murmured, her eyes glued to the screen. "Watch."

"He served in World War Two. In the merchant marines. Only he didn't go by Jack then."

Drew felt Tracy tense beside him. This was where it had started to get ugly. Groping for her hand, he hung on to it while her responses to Claire grew sharp and tense.

"I'm sorry," Claire said off camera, *"but I still*

*don't understand. You'll have to explain, Tracy.
Tell me who—"*

"*Tracy?*" The woman in the chair spit out a
curse. "*Jesus!*"

Her fingers dug into the suede chair arm. Anger
contorted her features.

"*Why do I have to go through this every time?
Why doesn't anyone believe me?*"

Mackenzie hit the Pause button. "Are you seeing
this? I want to make sure you're seeing this."

"We see it," Drew confirmed grimly.

He knew all too well what came next. Tracy
would shove out of her chair and storm across the
room. They'd confront each other, standing almost
nose-to-nose, until the sniper's bullet sent them
diving to the floor.

"Now watch!"

Mac switched to Play. The woman in the chair
resumed her angry dialogue.

The video cut to Drew. Caught him responding
with deliberate calm.

The video shot back to Tracy. Showed her in
profile, still planted in the chair, eyes squeezed shut.

Cut to Drew once more, all the way across the room.

Talking to empty air.

Chapter 15

Mac ran the composite video three more times from start to finish before Tracy, Drew and Claire accepted what was—or more correctly, wasn't—on it.

After the third showing, Mac clicked off the TV. Silence hung over the den like a dark, billowing thundercloud. Finally, Claire put into words the sick certainty Tracy had lived with for days now.

"How very remarkable. It appears there was another presence in the room with us."

Her calm acceptance of the unacceptable broke the dam. Drew swore, long and low. Mac tossed the remote end over end in her palm while bemoaning the fact her cameras hadn't captured a visual of the uninvited visitor. Tracy didn't know whether to whoop or cry with relief. She settled for jumping up and wrapping Mac in a fierce bear hug.

"Thank you!"

"For not capturing your ghost on video? You're welcome."

"But you saw her with your own eyes. All of you."

She spun around, giddy with the knowledge she wasn't the only one who now believed Trixie Halston constituted a real and ominous presence.

"You saw her and heard her and felt her."

"Yeah," Drew conceded, "we saw her."

Tracy knew how deep he'd had to dig for that admission. She also knew he didn't much like the fact that his head was now in sync with his gut.

"Okay, we all agree Trixie Halston is among us in some form or another," he said, scowling. "The question now is what the hell we're going to do about her."

His bald assumption that Trixie was their collective problem sent relief pouring through Tracy, but didn't surprise her. In the short time she and Drew had been together, he'd proved to be a take-charge man of action who got police detectives digging into old case files with one phone call and went charging after snipers.

"I know several professionals who've written papers on paranormal occurrences," Claire volunteered. "I'll make some calls tomorrow and get their recommendations on how we should best proceed."

"I'll go online and research more sophisticated equipment," Mac announced. "There's got to be *something* out there that will capture what we all experienced."

Tracy had her own ideas of what needed doing. "I think Drew and I should continue with our investigation into Trixie's death. She said she's just been drifting in a sort of emptiness until I took Jack's ashes to Catalina. That seemed to trigger the rage that brought her out."

"That and the belief Jack shoved her off a balcony," Drew concurred. "It sounds as if she can't—or won't—rest until she knows why."

"Or until we prove he didn't," Tracy countered stubbornly.

Claire had been thinking during their brief exchange. "You know, it seems to me there's another force at work here. Jack's death precipitated Tracy's visit to Catalina and, if she's correct, caused Trixie to manifest herself. But it was the *Kallister* that brought *us* to California."

The reminder that she'd been the object of an extensive undercover operation didn't particularly sit well with Tracy but struck a chord with Drew.

"Good point." He pushed to his feet and prowled the room. "The *Kallister* is the common thread running through time. That was Jack's ship. Trixie mentioned it in her last broadcast. She had a note in her pocket with the ship's name scribbled on it when she died. Sixty-five years later, Tracy's queries about the same vessel raise a red flag in Washington and send us hotfooting out here."

The three agents exchanged glances. When Tracy demanded to know what that look was all about, Drew sketched another scenario.

"We have to consider the possibility your queries about the *Kallister* also led to tonight's sniper attack."

"Why? How?"

"Think about it. Trixie admitted she'd heard rumors Jack was shipping out. She made a specific reference to the *Kallister* in a radio broadcast the night before the vessel weighed anchor. Forty nautical miles off the coast, it's torpedoed."

"I'm not following you. How do those events connect to me?"

"I think Trixie's reference to the *Kallister* had nothing to do with Jack. I think it was a signal that the ship was leaving port the next day. And I'm guessing that Japanese sub was lying in wait for her."

"Good Lord! Are you...? Are you saying Trixie Halston was a *spy?*"

"Yes."

Tracy's insides tightened. Her pulse started to race.

"The bloodstained note in Halston's pocket bugged me," Drew continued. "It struck me as too much of a coincidence that the same ship was torpedoed so soon after the singer's death, so I asked my contact at headquarters to run a list of all ships that had sailed from the same port as the *Kallister* six months before Halston made her swan dive."

The blood pounded in Tracy's ears like a runaway freight train. The beast clawed at her, a snarling creature that wanted to leap out and go for Drew's throat.

"This was prior to Pearl Harbor, remember. I knew some of our ships were attacked before the U.S. officially entered the war, but wasn't sure how many. Turns out five ships that sailed from the port of Los Angeles took hits."

The monster howled inside her now. She could feel its rage directed at Drew with enough force and energy to strip the skin from his flesh. She wouldn't let it out, wouldn't let it hurt him.

Relentless, he pounded another spike into its side. "After hearing Halston mention the *Kallister* in her last broadcast, I called headquarters again and asked them to dig into the Library of Congress radio archives. I wanted to know if she had tagged any of those five ships."

Nostrils flared, chest aching, Tracy struggled for breath. "Did…she?"

"Oh, yeah." His voice was as hard and as flat as his eyes. "The traitorous bitch tagged three."

The raging fury inside her went dead. Stone-cold dead.

"Noooo!"

The shriek ripped from her throat.

"I didn't do that! I couldn't have! Not to Johnny!"

Her eyes rolled back. The room went black. With an anguished moan, she toppled to the floor.

"Tracy. Sweetheart."

Drew fought to keep the panic from his voice. Battling the urge to crush her against him, he cradled her gently in his arms. Her skin felt like ice. Her breathing was so slow and shallow he found himself holding his own until his lungs screamed for air.

She'd been out for a good five minutes. Mac had raced upstairs for a blanket, which was now swaddled around the unconscious woman. Claire squatted beside the sofa and monitored her pulse. Drew held her close and tried to pull her from the darkness by the sheer force of his will.

"Tracy, can you hear me?"

Her eyelids twitched. A frown creased her forehead. Relief crashed through Drew.

"C'mon, Tracy. Come out of it. You're safe. I've got you."

The lies tasted like sewer water in his mouth. She wasn't safe. He could shove her out of the path of a sniper's bullet but couldn't protect her from the creature that tore at her mind and body. He'd never felt so damned frustrated or helpless in his life.

"Drew?"

Her lids fluttered up. Her dazed eyes slowly focused, then lit with fear.

"Are you all right?"

"I'm fine. You're the one who keeled over."

Either she didn't hear him or didn't believe him. Dragging an arm free of the blanket, she patted his cheek with a frantic hand.

"She didn't get to you? She didn't hurt you?"

"I'm okay."

"Thank God!" She collapsed against his chest, shuddering. "I wouldn't let her out. She wanted at you in the worst way, but I wouldn't let her out."

Christ! *She'd* protected him.

The realization hit Drew at the same time it did the other two women. Admiration flitted across Claire's delicate features. Mac gave a low whistle.

"Way to go, Trace. You just went a couple rounds with a poltergeist and won."

"I don't feel like I won," she whispered raggedly, still wracked by tremors. "She sucked me dry. I ache all the way down to my bones."

Humbled by her courage and shaken to *his* bones by her utter exhaustion, Drew scooped her into his arms.

"Let's get you to bed."

She didn't protest. Limp as a rag doll, she let him carry her upstairs. But when he yanked back the covers and eased her onto the mattress, the fear she battled so valiantly to suppress broke the surface.

"Stay with me. Just for tonight. Please."

"I'm not going anywhere."

He removed her shoes and dropped them beside

the bed. His thumped down a moment later. He hit
the light switch and plunged the room into darkness.
Stretching out, he tucked her against him and
dragged the covers up to her chin.

He didn't pull in a full breath until he heard hers
even out. Even then he couldn't relax. He remained
awake long after she'd drifted into sleep, fiercely determined to keep her ghost away without knowing
just how the hell he'd do it.

Tracy woke the next morning to hazy sunshine
and the high-pitched trill of a bird outside the
window. She lay still, cushioned against Drew's
shoulder, until he sensed her conscious state.

"'Morning."

His breath was a warm wash against her temple.
His calloused palm stroked her hair.

"How do you feel?"

"Pretty much like those shrimp we tossed overboard. Nibbled to death."

"Think a cup of coffee might cure those nibbles?
I heard Claire and Mac go downstairs a while ago.
They've probably got a pot brewing."

"I'd kill for coffee."

"Don't move."

"Like I could."

The warm, hard pillow slipped away. Her head
plopped onto a much softer one as Drew rolled out
of bed. He looked about like she felt. Bristles

darkened his cheeks, his hair lay flat as a board on one side and his shirttails hung in wrinkled folds.

Watching him roll his neck and stretch his cramped muscles made Tracy's own muscles coil. She hadn't forgiven him for deceiving her. Or thinking she might have been collecting information on a U.S. naval vessel for some ulterior purpose. That still stung.

Yet her single, driving need last night had been to shield him from Trixie's vituperative wrath when he accused the dead singer of being a spy. Like a lynx protecting her injured mate, Tracy had hissed and spit and used her claws to force Trixie back into her cage.

She'd do it again. In a heartbeat.

Rolling over, Tracy buried her face in his pillow and breathed in his scent while she battled an increasingly urgent need to hit the bathroom. When she couldn't ignore it any longer, she dragged back the covers.

Her most pressing need attended to, she washed her hands and face in the sculpted sink. She barely recognized the hollow eyes and haggard face staring back at her in the mirror above the vanity. At least the clothes she'd rinsed out the night before had dried.

Feeling almost human again, Tracy was on her way out of the bathroom when Drew returned. He'd splashed some water on his face, too, and raked his fingers through his hair, but his shirttail still flapped around his thighs.

"Here you go. Cream, no sugar."

"Thank you."

She took the mug in both hands, absurdly moved that he remembered how she took her coffee. As best she could recall, they'd shared only one cup in the café next to the Avalon Casino museum.

Okay, maybe she could forgive his deception. Excusing him for thinking she might be a traitor would take a little more time.

Traitor.

The echo ricocheted inside her head. Her chest squeezed, not with rage, not with fury, but with silent, unbearable sadness.

"Trixie didn't tag those ships, Drew."

His head came up. Eyes narrowed, he studied her through the spiraling steam. "How do you know?"

"I just do."

"We've got her on tape, sweetheart. The Library of Congress located eight different 1941 broadcasts featuring the Kenny Jones Orchestra. Trixie singled out five specific ships. Three of those vessels took torpedoes. This is more than a case of loose lips sinking ships."

"I know that."

"Security ratcheted up exponentially after Pearl Harbor," Drew said, his jaw tight. "Someone would have tumbled to her, sooner rather than later. Maybe someone already had. Maybe that's why she took a dive."

"You've heard her, Drew! She didn't jump. She was pushed."

The rage that had ripped through Tracy was too real, the anguish too deep. Cradling her coffee with both hands, she pleaded Trixie's case.

"Halston may have mentioned the vessels on-air, but she didn't do it with intent to cause harm. She said as much last night. She wouldn't do that. Not to Jack. Someone must have fed her that information and used her as a mouthpiece."

"Someone undoubtedly did." Drew's face hardened. "I'm guessing it was the same someone who left his fingerprint on that bloodstained note."

"Ed LaSorta?"

"Ed LaSorta."

"What does that fingerprint prove? Ed could have just handed Trixie a note someone else passed to him."

"I might buy that, if a professional hit man hadn't taken a shot at you."

"You said last night it was all linked. Trixie's death. My queries about the *Kallister*. The sniper. But I can't... Oh, my God!"

In a starburst of light, she saw herself standing in LaSorta's office. Smiling down at the man. Swearing she was going to keep digging until she solved the riddle of Trixie's death.

"You think Ed LaSorta hired a hit man because he tagged the ships all those years ago and was afraid I would now tag *him?*"

"I think it's a damned good possibility."

"But...but LaSorta and the band toured with the

USO! I saw the pictures in his office, taken right at the front lines. They were in uniforms and helmets. How could he betray his country, then turn around and risk his life to entertain troops?"

"I've had folks up all night digging into LaSorta's background. Turns out he joined the America First Committee in early 1941, along with a host of others that included Charles Lindbergh, Lillian Gish, Sinclair Lewis and idealistic young students like Gore Vidal and our future president, Gerald Ford. At its peak, the AFC had some 800,000 members, all vehemently opposed to the U.S. entering the war in Europe."

"I've never heard of the AFC."

"Neither had I. Probably because it disbanded just days after Pearl Harbor and most of the members subsequently joined the U.S. war effort."

"Like LaSorta."

"Exactly. Prior to Pearl Harbor, though, the AFC held massive antiwar rallies and marches. It also attracted some pretty radical fringe elements suspected of bombing recruiting stations and sabotaging shipments of supplies intended for the Brits and their allies. They justified their actions by asserting Roosevelt violated the 1939 Neutrality Act when he pushed the lend-lease program through Congress. They believed he was dragging the country willy-nilly into war."

Tracy sank onto the edge of the bed, cursing when coffee slopped all over her clean sweater. Her mind whirled as she tried to grasp the unbelievable series of events tying her to acts of treason that happened more than sixty years ago.

"It's hard to see LaSorta as one of those young radicals."

"Now it is," Drew agreed. "Not so hard if you put him in the context of those prewar years. That's the tack Claire and I are going to take when we talk to him this morning, anyway."

"Claire and you?"

"Mac will stay here with you."

"I don't think so."

"You're safe here. No one followed us last night. We made sure of that."

Tracy had already spilled most of her coffee down her front. She set what was left aside, resisting the temptation to dump it over Drew's head. She'd do it, though, if that's what it took to get through to him.

"First, you're not brushing me aside like a pesky puppy. Second, I've got as much or more invested in this op as you have. Third—"

"Op?" he interrupted, amusement leaking through the hard cast of his face.

"That's what Claire called it. Third, Trixie will rip out your throat if you try to leave her behind. She needs to hear what LaSorta has to say. More to the point, she needs to know once and for all Jack didn't kill her."

"I'll agree to let you come along on one condition."

That "let" had her bristling, but she heard him out.

"LaSorta won't be expecting us and most likely won't have any other hired guns around. But there's always a chance things could get dicey. If anything— *anything*—unexpected occurs, you do what I tell you, when I tell you. No questions, no hesitation. Agreed?"

"Agreed."

"All right. Get changed. I'll meet you downstairs."

He left her contemplating her soggy front and wondering what the heck she'd change into. Luckily, Mac rapped on her door as she was pawing through her weekender.

"Drew said you were up. He also said you'd spilled your coffee. I brought you another cup."

"Bless you."

She set the mug on the bedside table and eyed the jumbled pile Tracy was digging through.

"Run out of clean clothes?"

"Two days ago. You wouldn't happen to have a clean shirt I could borrow?"

"I think I can fix you up. Come with me."

Mac insisted on supplying more than a shirt. After outfitting Tracy with a black turtleneck and slim-hipped slacks, she threaded a thin rope studded with Swarovski crystals in a tiger-striped pattern through the belt loops.

"Now for your hair. Best to sweep it up and out of your face when you're going into the field. You don't want to restrict your field of vision. Sit."

Wielding hairbrush and clip, Mac caught the heavy

mass up in a loose twist and anchored it with a jumbo clip studded with the same sparkling crystals.

From there they progressed to eye shadow in a muted taupe, to cut the glare so she wouldn't lose the target in bright light, and raspberry lip gloss, because Mac liked the taste.

Tracy couldn't help but appreciate the irony as she descended the stairs some time later. In the past week she'd assumed personas that ranged from mousy number-cruncher to glamorous big band singer to superchic secret agent. She liked this one best.

Feeling like Angelina Jolie in *Mr. and Mrs. Smith,* she breezed down the stairs.

Chapter 16

Tracy's breezy self-confidence lasted only until she, Drew and the others pulled up at Edward LaSorta's Laguna Beach residence.

Her palms started to sweat when Drew rang the bell and informed the maid Mr. LaSorta was expecting them. Her stomach did the hip-hop all the way down a long entryhall and into a monstrous living room with high, vaulted ceilings and a magnificent view of the sea.

"Mr. LaSorta's with his physical therapist," the maid relayed. "I'll let him know you're here."

"Thanks."

The oceanfront residence was built on three stair-stepping levels that jutted out over the rocky coast. The entry level contained the kitchen, a dining room and the living room. Above, a series of what Tracy assumed were the bedrooms opened off the railed balcony. Another wooden railing separated the middle level from the lower portion of the house.

Nervous as a cat, Tracy followed the rhythmic clank of weights to the railing. Below her was a workout room with a mirrored wall, massage tables and a universal gym that would make a professional bodybuilder proud. She caught a glimpse via the mirror of a muscular attendant watching closely while the white-maned LaSorta pumped iron.

No wonder the bastard looked so good for his age!

A flicker of movement announced the maid's arrival. The clanking ceased. LaSorta swiped his face with the towel draped around his neck, released the brakes on his wheelchair and moved out of sight.

More nervous by the moment, Tracy clutched the rail and shifted her gaze to the view outside the tall, tinted windows. Waves foamed against the cliffs and crags of the coast. A haze of smog hung over the sea in the near distance. Farther out, she saw with a sudden hitch in her breath, rose the gray blur of Catalina Island.

Her lungs squeezed, cutting off all air. Her heart seemed to stop, then kick-started again with a painful thump.

The gray blur filled her vision. The rest of the

world faded. The island called to her. Taunted her. Lured her.

She leaned forward. The railing pressed into her hips. Her blood thundered in her ears, so loud she barely heard the whir of the chairlift that announced LaSorta's arrival.

"What's so important you had to interrupt my morning therapy, McDowell?"

The irritated query spun Tracy around. Her heart hammering, she watched LaSorta wheel off the lift and into the living room.

This wasn't the affable, pin-striped exec who'd greeted them two days ago. Sweat ringed the armpits of his workout shirt. The white towel draped around his neck gave his face a grayish cast. The leathery skin had folded in on itself, carving deep canyons in his cheeks, and his smile wasn't as welcoming as he took in Claire and Mac's presence.

"Who are these people?"

"Associates of mine," Drew answered, equally terse. "We want to talk to you about your involvement in the AFC."

"The American Film Center?"

"The America First Committee."

Surprise blanked LaSorta's face. Either he was one heck of an actor or he honestly didn't know the reason for this unplanned visit.

"I haven't heard anyone mention the committee in fifty, sixty years."

"You were a member, weren't you?"

"Yes, I was. So were half the musicians and artists I worked with. None of us wanted to go over and fight Europe's war."

LaSorta's glance cut to Tracy, who stood frozen beside the rail. She felt something stir inside her, recognized the sensation instantly.

Oh, God! Not now. Please, not now.

"I'm not ashamed of joining the AFC," LaSorta asserted, shifting his attention back to Drew. "We didn't know about Hitler's death camps or the massacres in Manchuria. Not then. We honestly believed the war in Europe wasn't our war. And it *wasn't*, until FDR provoked the attack on Pearl Harbor and dragged us into the damned thing."

"Provoked?" Drew echoed softly.

The tremors inside Tracy gathered power and force. Trixie was there, wanting out, demanding a role in the unfolding drama. Tracy held her in by sheer strength of will as LaSorta dredged up long-forgotten politics.

"Of course Roosevelt provoked the Japanese attack! He didn't know when it would come, maybe, or where, but the Japanese had to cut off the flow of supplies going to the Aussies and Chinese. Every ship sailing from the port of Los Angeles with munitions or war materials waved a red flag in Tojo's face."

"So you decided to help stop that flow."

LaSorta's cloudy blue eyes narrowed. "What the hell are you talking about?"

"Trixie Halston singled out a U.S. munitions ship during her sign-off the night she died."

"Best I recall, she singled out a number of ships in her sign-offs. I told you the sailors were always sniffing around her skirts. Mentioning their ships was her way of stringing them along. She made every one of 'em think she sang to him alone, that she loved him and would wait until he got back from wherever he was shipping out to. Fat chance of that," he added with a sneer. "Trixie Halston didn't love anyone but Trixie Halston."

Fury ripped at Tracy's insides, raking her with nails as sharp as claws. She had to fight to hear Drew over the roaring in her ears.

"The ship Halston mentioned the night she died left the port of Los Angeles the next morning and was torpedoed forty miles off the coast."

"I remember. That was terrible. Terrible. Like I said, those ships were a red flag, taunting the Japanese to take them out. What does any of this have to do with me?"

"The police found a note in Halston's pocket with the name of that ship scribbled in pencil."

"I heard something about a note. No one attached any significance to it at the time. We figured it was just to jog her memory for the sign-off, in case she was spaced out. She usually was."

The rage inside Tracy burst into a thousand icy splinters. She couldn't hold it back now, didn't even try as Drew hammered at the aged PR exec.

"Your fingerprints were on that note, LaSorta."

"The hell you say!"

The man's face went almost as gray as his sweats. His Adam's apple bobbed above the white towel. Gripping his chair arms, he recovered swiftly.

"If the police had any suspicions about that note *or* found my prints on it, they would have questioned me at the time of Trixie's death."

"They lifted a print, but didn't have one to match it to at the time. Detective Riley at LAPD reran it for me two days ago. This time it popped up in the system. You shouldn't have been shooting up at that party in the mid-sixties, LaSorta."

"So I touched the friggin' note sixty years ago? Someone in the audience must have passed it to me to give her. Hell, there were upwards of three thousand people on the dance floor that night. It could have been anyone."

"Liar!"

The explosive accusation whipped everyone's head around, including Drew's. His heart jumped into his throat when he recognized the snarling female who raged at LaSorta.

"You wrote that note, Eddie! You passed it to me. Just like you passed me the others."

"What the hell…?"

Drew and Claire stood frozen. Mac cursed under her breath, wishing to hell she had a camera to record this. Tracy—Trixie—advanced on the man in the wheelchair.

"Now I know why you'd pumped me for information about Johnny's ship."

LaSorta's eyes bugged.

"You got me to tell you he was shipping out, didn't you? You passed me that note to remind me to wish him a safe passage on air, didn't you? Then you turned all kinds of green when I let drop that I'd asked him to meet me because I had something urgent to tell him. *Didn't you?*"

"I…I…" His mouth agape, LaSorta gasped for air. "I don't know what you're talking about."

"You thought I'd tipped him to what you were doing? God almighty, I should have! You practically frothed at the mouth whenever anyone brought up the war and the possibility of a draft."

"You're crazy! I want you out of my house. All of you. Get out!"

Ignoring his frantic demands, she prowled toward him, step by menacing step.

"You knew you'd be one of the first called up. No wife. No kids. No vices except booze and drugs. And a yellow streak a mile wide down your back."

Eyes wild, hands pumping, LaSorta wheeled away from her. Relentless, she stalked him, circled him, tormented him.

"That was you, out there on the balcony. All this time I thought it was Johnny, but it was you. You shoved me, Eddie. You killed me."

"Get back!" His chair crashed into a side table. "Get away!"

"You killed me, you slimy little bastard. Now I'll haunt you for the rest of your pathetic life. You'll see me every day. Hear me every hour of every night."

Smiling viciously, she started to sing. Low, throaty, in Trixie Halston's unmistakable, inimitable style.

Every note hit LaSorta like an open-handed slap to the face. He jerked in his chair, twisting and turning to escape the blows.

Drew couldn't let it go on. Whatever the hell he'd done, the man had rights. "That's enough," he said sharply, grabbing Tracy's arm.

"No!" She shook loose and kept LaSorta pinned in her relentless glare. "That's not nearly enough! I want him to suffer. I want to break every bone in his body, like he broke mine. I want…"

She broke off, her eyes widening as a now hysterical LaSorta yanked open the table drawer.

"I killed you once, you bitch. Maybe this time you'll stay dead."

In the split second that followed, everything happened at once. Mac shouted a warning.

Drew whirled, shoving Trixie behind him.

Claire lunged for the man in the chair.

And Tracy reclaimed her mind and her body and

her heart. Throwing herself sideways, she pulled LaSorta's fire away from Drew.

The force of the bullet knocked her into the railing. Wood splintered. Her arms flailed empty air.

As she plunged through the rail, her frantic eyes locked on the gray bulk of Catalina Island.

"No!" Her last scream spiraled into howling fury. "Not again!"

With superhuman effort, she twisted in midair at the same time something—someone?—snagged her belt.

Epilogue

The liquid notes soared through the bright California sunshine. The golden slide of two trombones in perfect unison gave way to the reedy seduction of a sax and the swish of a steel brush against the cymbals. Lost to the dreamy melody, more than two hundred couples swayed across the parquet floor of the Avalon Ballroom.

After the first refrain, the singer stepped to the mike. In a velvet voice reminiscent of Dinah Shore and Billie Holliday, she crooned the lyrics to "I'll Walk Alone."

"You sure you're okay with that song?"

Tracy's cheek brushed the shiny satin lapels of her groom's tux. Lifting her head, she smiled up at him.

"Very okay."

"No goose bumps or shivery sensations?"

"Not a one. Trixie's happy now. Me, too," she added with a silly grin.

She should be.

A broken Edward LaSorta had confessed every-thing and was now the second oldest convict in the California prison system. The USS *Kallister* had returned from whatever secret mission it had been sent on and sat at anchor at the Port of Los Angeles.

And Drew had proposed after flatly refusing to leave Tracy's side during her long weeks of recovery and rehab.

The bullet had nicked her lung. She was lucky it hadn't killed her. Even luckier that the thin, crystal-studded belt Mac loaned her had caught on a jagged spindle of the broken railing, halting her plunge to the workout room below.

That's what Drew said happened, anyway. She knew better. That narrow belt didn't save her from a fatal fall. Trixie did.

Which is why Tracy had accepted an invitation from Claire's associate to serve as a consultant with the International Institute for Paranormal Studies. Every day her work opened exciting new vistas in her mind—and Drew's.

The hefty consulting fees the institute paid her weren't bad, either. They more than covered the cost of her hand-sewn wedding dress in rich, creamy satin and the pearl-studded snood holding back the heavy mass of her hair. They even covered the cost of the honeymoon suite at the Bella Vista Inn.

But Drew's friends had insisted on taking care of this lavish wedding reception. Nick's L.A. catered the affair, under the watchful eye of its tall, handsome owner. Claire and her gorgeous husband, Luis Esteban, hired the orchestra. Charlie, Drew's business partner and ex-father-in-law, had furnished the flowers that graced every table, insisting Tracy was now a daughter of sorts.

She glanced around the room, her heart swelling. She'd come to Catalina six months ago alone, out of a job and devastated by Jack's death. Now she shared this day and this beautiful ballroom with a host of new friends, an adopted father-in-law and Drew.

Leaning back in his arms, she let her happiness shine in her voice. "Have I told you lately that I love you?"

"Not since I put that ring on your finger 'bout an hour ago."

"Then I'd better tell you again. Or better yet, I'll sing it to you."

Smiling, she hooked her wrists around his neck. The notes came from her heart, light and clear.

I'll always be near you, wherever you are
Each night, in every prayer.
If you call me, I'll hear you, no matter how far—
Just close your eyes, and I'll be there.

* * *

A breeze drifted through the open doors leading to the balcony. A soft sigh, shimmering with joy, floated with it.

Johnny!

* * * * *

New York Times *bestselling author*
Linda Lael Miller is back with a new romance
featuring the heartwarming McKettrick family
from Silhouette Special Edition.

SIERRA'S HOMECOMING
by Linda Lael Miller

On sale December 2006,
wherever books are sold.

Turn the page for a sneak preview!

New York Times *bestselling author*
Linda Lael Miller is back with a new romance
featuring the heartwarming McKettrick family
from Silhouette Special Edition.

SIERRA'S HOMECOMING
by Linda Lael Miller

On sale December 2006,
wherever books are sold.

Turn the page for a sneak preview!

Soft, smoky music poured into the room.

The next thing she knew, Sierra was in Travis's arms, close against that chest she'd admired earlier, and they were slow dancing.

Why didn't she pull away?

"Relax," he said. His breath was warm in her hair.

She giggled, more nervous than amused. What was the matter with her? She was attracted to Travis, had been from the first, and he was clearly attracted to her. They were both adults. Why not enjoy a little slow dancing in a ranch-house kitchen?

Because slow dancing led to other things. She took a step back and felt the counter flush against her lower back. Travis naturally came with her, since they were holding hands and he had one arm around her waist.

Simple physics.

Then he kissed her.

Physics again—this time, not so simple.

"Yikes," she said, when their mouths parted.

He grinned. "Nobody's ever said that after I kissed them."

She felt the heat and substance of his body pressed against hers. "It's going to happen, isn't it?" she heard herself whisper.

"Yep," Travis answered.

"But not tonight," Sierra said on a sigh.

"Probably not," Travis agreed.

"When, then?"

He chuckled, gave her a slow, nibbling kiss. "Tomorrow morning," he said. "After you drop Liam off at school."

"Isn't that…a little…soon?"

"Not soon enough," Travis answered, his voice husky. "Not nearly soon enough."

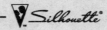

HARLEQUIN® *Romance*®

**From the Heart.
For the Heart.**

*Get swept away into the Outback
with two of Harlequin Romance's
top authors.*

Coming in December...

Claiming the
Cattleman's Heart
BY BARBARA HANNAY

And in January don't miss...

Outback Man Seeks Wife
BY MARGARET WAY

REQUEST YOUR FREE BOOKS!

2 FREE NOVELS
PLUS 2 FREE GIFTS!

Silhouette® Romantic

SUSPENSE

Sparked by Danger, Fueled by Passion!

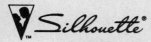

Silhouette®
Romantic
SUSPENSE

**From *New York Times*
bestselling author Maggie Shayne**

When Selene comes to the aid of an unconscious stranger,
she doesn't expect to be accused of harming him. The
handsome stranger's amnesia doesn't help her cause either.
Determined to find out what really happened to Cory,
the two end up on an intense ride of dangerous pasts
and the search for a ruthless killer.

DANGEROUS LOVER #1443
December 2006

Available wherever you buy books.

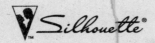

COMING NEXT MONTH

#1443 DANGEROUS LOVER—Maggie Shayne
The Oklahoma All-Girl Brands
When an attempted murder leaves a victim with amnesia, he seeks the help of his attractive rescuer to piece together his dangerous past—but can he trust this bewitching woman and potential suspect?

#1444 FROM MISSION TO MARRIAGE—Lyn Stone
Special Ops
A killer returns to claim his revenge, and as the chase heats up, so does Special Ops agent Clay Senate's desire for his new tall, sexy and all-too-feminine hire.

#1445 WARRIOR'S SECOND CHANCE—Nancy Gideon
To rescue her family, Barbara D'Angelo turns to the man she left behind years ago, and soon uncovers a decades-old wrong hidden behind a maze of false memories.

#1446 RULES OF RE-ENGAGEMENT—Loreth Anne White
Shadow Soldiers
Presumed dead, a wanted man returns to his country to overthrow a terrorist leader...but to do so he must reunite with the only woman he's ever loved—his enemy's daughter.

SIMCNM1106